WHEN A COWBOY FALLS HARD

THE BRIDGER BUNCH

Vicki Lewis Thompson

Ocean Dance Press

WHEN A COWBOY FALLS HARD

ISBN: 978-1-63803-865-8

Ocean Dance Press LLC
PO Box 69901
Oro Valley, AZ 85737

Visit the author's website at
VickiLewisThompson.com

"I'll bet this isn't the first time Tex has latched onto a random adult."

"Actually, it is." Zinnia finally looked at him. "His social life in Great Falls consisted of the kids at his pre-school and their parents. None of the dads were cowboys."

"Do you think that's all it is? The outfit?"

"It's the outfit, but it's also your job. You take care of horses. And there's your ranch, and your, um—" She licked her lips and gestured toward him. "Your mannerisms."

Her lower lip glistened where she'd run her tongue over it. Monty sucked in air. "I don't have mannerisms."

"It's your walk, the way you stand, the tilt of your hat, the tone of your voice...." She trailed off, her gaze locked with his.

His heartbeat was out of control. "Are we..." He paused to clear his throat. "Are we still talking about your kid?"

"Yes. No." She dragged in a breath. "Look, you don't want to get tangled up with me."

"You're right, I don't."

"See, I knew that. You're not ready for—"

"I'm not. But—"

"Then we're on the same page."

"Meaning we want each other?"

"Meaning it's a terrible idea."

Want more cowboys? Check out these other titles by Vicki Lewis Thompson

The Bridger Bunch

When a Cowboy Takes Charge
When a Cowboy Tempts Fate
When a Cowboy Skips Christmas
When a Cowboy Falls Hard

Rowdy Ranch

Having the Cowboy's Baby
Stoking the Cowboy's Fire
Testing the Cowboy's Resolve
Rocking the Cowboy's Christmas
Roping the Cowboy's Heart
Tempting the Cowboy's Sister
Craving the Cowboy's Kiss
Heating Up the Cowboy's Christmas
Wrangling the Cowboy's Dreams
Blowing the Cowboy's Mind
Finding the Cowboy's Family
Saving the Cowboy's Christmas

The Buckskin Brotherhood

Sweet-Talking Cowboy
Big-Hearted Cowboy
Baby-Daddy Cowboy
True-Blue Cowboy
Strong-Willed Cowboy
Secret-Santa Cowboy
Stand-Up Cowboy
Single-Dad Cowboy
Marriage-Minded Cowboy
Gift-Giving Cowboy

The McGavin Brothers
A Cowboy's Strength
A Cowboy's Honor
A Cowboy's Return
A Cowboy's Heart
A Cowboy's Courage
A Cowboy's Christmas
A Cowboy's Kiss
A Cowboy's Luck
A Cowboy's Charm
A Cowboy's Challenge
A Cowboy's Baby
A Cowboy's Holiday
A Cowboy's Choice
A Cowboy's Worth
A Cowboy's Destiny
A Cowboy's Secret
A Cowboy's Homecoming

Urban Cowboys
The Trailblazer
The Drifter
The Lawman

1

Fighting a mild headache, Monty Bridger shrugged into a denim jacket, left his cottage and headed for the barn to meet his mom. A warm breeze caressed his freshly shaven jaw. He could've skipped the jacket.

He paused to draw in a cleansing breath. The bright aroma of new growth and loamy, fertile earth was so strong he could almost taste it.

Raindrops from an early morning shower sparkled on blades of grass poking up in his front yard. A stand of pines to his right glittered as if they'd been strung with fairy lights.

His headache eased. God, he loved this ranch, especially in June, and not just because he had a birthday coming up in two days. This was the time of year folks in Montana greeted with relief and joy.

Then again, he enjoyed all four seasons. The predictable shift from one to the next kept things interesting. He was good with that level of change in his life.

But abrupt and unexpected changes made him nervous. Which explained his headache this morning. He adjusted the fit of his Stetson and continued down the gentle slope toward the barn.

His mom waited for him by the open barn doors. From this distance she could be mistaken for a teenager dressed in jeans and a sweatshirt, especially with her salt and pepper hair tucked under her Stetson.

She'd been his rock the past couple of years, grounding him and the rest of the family as they'd navigated life without their dad. She was the strongest person he'd ever known.

As he approached, he listened for the distinctive rumble of Graham's new truck on the ranch road. Couldn't hear it yet.

"Hey, *mijo*." His mom gave him a smile. "Were you gathering your forces just now?"

He returned her smile. "More or less. Nice choice on the sweatshirt." Luis's wife Jordan had given one to each of them for Christmas—bright green with *Bridger Bunch* across the front.

She nudged back her hat and gazed up at him. "Figured it would be a fun thing to wear when we meet our new farrier. I wondered if you'd do the same and we'd be matchy-matchy."

"Mine's in the wash."

"Might be just as well. One sweatshirt is folksy. Two is more of a statement. Graham said his niece is freaked out about shoeing our horses since we're his oldest and biggest account."

"I'm a little freaked out, myself. Graham Harrison's been shoeing our horses as long as I can remember."

"Same here. He was the ranch's farrier when I married your dad."

"It's gonna be strange having someone else do it."

"I suppose, but it's not like he's retiring. He'll work alongside her, especially at first."

"Are you positive he's not sick or something?" He winced as pain jabbed at his temple.

"*Si, mijo*. I grilled him about his health. He says he's fine."

"Do you believe him?"

"I do. I threatened to make his life a living hell if he was lying to me."

"Then I don't get why he's taking on an assistant. He's never said the work is getting too hard, at least not to me."

"He's not the complaining type."

"Do you think he needs the help?"

"Possibly. He's the same age as your dad." Her breath caught. "Or the age your dad would've been." She cleared her throat. "It's a physically demanding job."

"Are you *sure* he's not sick?"

"I'm sure." She gazed at him. "He knew why I was quizzing him. He's been a fixture around here."

"That's putting it mildly. Thanks to him, I'm a better vet. He's taught me to look for things I might have missed."

"And he's likely passed those tips on to his niece."

"Makes sense." He let out a sigh. "What's her name again?"

"Zinnia."

"Like the flower?"

"Like the flower. Graham says she really knows her stuff."

"He's her uncle. He might be prejudiced."

"Yes, but he loves this family. He wouldn't saddle us with a farrier who doesn't measure up."

"Something just occurred to me. Graham's brother died years ago. Is Zinnia—"

"Yeah, that was her dad. He crashed the family's small plane. Her mom died, too."

"Ouch. When was that?"

"Let me think. You were a senior, so ten years ago. They lived in Great Falls. The girls were in college. He's kept in close touch with them ever since."

"Then this could be about giving his niece a boost instead of him needing a hand."

"Possibly. I don't know all the details, but Zinnia has a—" At the sound of a truck, she paused to glance toward the road. "That'll be them."

"Yep." Seconds later a four-door pickup with a deluxe red paint job appeared around the bend. It cruised slowly down the rain-dampened dirt road, its grill shining in the sun. "Looks like he doesn't want to get mud on his fancy truck."

His mom laughed. "Never thought I'd see the day when he worried about that."

"I still can't believe he bought a bright red one."

"He blames it on a mid-life crisis."

"Oh? Do you think he'll start dating?"

"Huh." His mom paused. "I didn't think of that, but maybe. When Adele left he said he was through with women, but I guess anything's possible."

Monty heaved a sigh of relief. When he'd been obsessing about Graham's decision to cut back, he hadn't taken the new truck into account. He should have. A dying man wouldn't buy himself a lipstick-red Cowboy Cadillac.

But if that man had healed from a nasty divorce and hankered for some company, he might decide a snazzy new truck was in order.

By the time Graham had backed into his usual spot near the barn, Monty's headache was gone. He and his mom walked toward the truck as Graham hopped out with his usual vigor and rounded the hood.

He didn't look the least bit sick. The guy was in his prime, still in good shape....

Uh-oh. Speaking of good shape....

Zinnia.

Her descent from the passenger side put pressure on his eyeballs and glued his tongue to the roof of his mouth. He'd never been face-to-face with a more voluptuous woman, especially one wearing steel-toed boots.

She'd chosen the same kind of outfit as her uncle—plaid long-sleeved shirt tucked into sturdy jeans and a baseball cap tugged low over her eyes. But the clothes he'd seen Graham wear hundreds of times produced a totally different effect on an hour-glass figure that nearly brought him to his knees. Holy moly.

She was tall, at least five-ten in those boots, and she moved with the grace of an athlete. Toned muscles flexed beneath her shirt and jeans as she came toward him. His dazed brain processed her stride in slow motion so he wouldn't miss a thing.

Was he already mentally undressing her? Seemed like it. She'd pulled her blonde curly hair through the back of her Anvil Brand cap. Hoping she hadn't noticed him ogling, he focused on her ponytail swinging in time with each step.

He itched to tug off that cap and set those ringlets free. Then he'd—

Stop it, dumbass! Look her in the eye.

But the hat brim shaded her eyes. He was forced to concentrate on her smiling lips—pale pink, plump and extremely kissable. Near as he could tell, she wore no makeup.

She and her uncle stopped a few feet away and Graham started making introductions.

Monty's nostrils flared as he breathed in the scent of citrus blended with freshly washed cotton. And something else, a subtle aroma that sent a message straight to his privates. He was in big trouble.

Thank God her attention was on his mother. Maybe she hadn't noticed the hot mess she'd created in his body. Then she glanced his way, laughter dancing in green eyes the color of a willow in spring.

Busted. Heat rose from the collar of his shirt and his jacket became uncomfortably warm.

What was wrong with him? This wasn't his first rodeo. He'd never ever laid eyes on a woman he'd just met and instantly imagined taking her to bed.

Until now. Until Zinnia. Graham could've warned him. No, he couldn't have. That would have been creepy.

He'd have to own his reaction. Nothing about her dress or manner was deliberately seductive. That was a blessing. One sultry look from her and he'd likely lose what was left of his mind.

She shook hands with his mom. "I can't believe I'm finally here. Uncle Graham's talked about you and the Bridger Bunch for years."

"I hope he didn't oversell us."

"No worries, Raquel." Graham chuckled. "I've been around too long for that. I know you're not perfect, but you're damn good people."

"Thanks. So are you. Welcome to Laughing Creek, Zinnia. Monty and I look forward to working with you."

"Absolutely." Monty had used the time to covertly wipe his sweaty palm on his jacket. "Nice to meet you, Zinnia." He offered his hand and hoped for the best.

"Nice to meet you, Monty." Her gaze was steady and her grasp was firm. No moisture. "Is Monty short for Montana?"

"No, ma'am. Montgomery."

"Ah. I hear you're a good vet."

"I do my best." He let go of her, but it took effort. Her touch was magnetic. He wanted to grab hold and never let go. He wanted—

"I'm in need of a good vet."

"You are?" Wincing at the eager lilt in his voice, he cleared his throat. "You have a horse?" *Great question. Of course she does, genius.*

"A pregnant mare. According to my vet in Great Falls, she's due any day. It's her first foal. Trailering her down here was a risk but we made it without incident. And now I need—"

"Of course." He jumped in, then took a breath. "Sorry. What would you like me to do?"

"If you'd drop by and check on her, that would be wonderful. Uncle Graham calls you Supervet."

"It's a joke."

Graham laughed. "Not really."

"Anyway, I think she's close, but I'd like an expert opinion."

And he was way too eager to give it. He did his best to sound nonchalant. "I might be able to take a look this afternoon, depending on your schedule." Yeah, not nonchalant. But come on — a gorgeous woman and a mare ready to foal? Kryptonite.

"This is our only gig today so after we're done, it would be great if you could come over. I understand you mostly work with Laughing Creek horses, and I will contact the other vet in town if you're too busy to take her on as a patient, but—"

"I'll be glad to help. I can work her in." His mom was watching him with interest. Naturally she was. He might as well have painted his intentions on his forehead.

"Awesome. Uncle Graham thought you might make an exception for Speckles since you also do the wellness checks on his horses as a special favor."

"Is Speckles an Appaloosa?"

She nodded. "Leopard Appy. She's a sweetie. I really appreciate this, and to be clear, I'm paying you."

No, she wasn't, but he wouldn't say that now. "Okay, but let's discuss the details later. The horses heard you drive up and they're getting antsy. Ready to meet them?"

"Can't wait."

"I need to excuse myself from the walk-through today," his mom said. "Adam and I have something to discuss before he heads into town. Monty, would you come on up when you're done? We could use your input, too."

"Will do."

"Oh, and Graham." She turned in his direction. "Can you guys stay for lunch? I was planning on it since we always do that, but if you and Zinnia—"

"Lunch would be fantastic. Theoretically we'll finish earlier with two of us, but I'll be giving Zin additional background as we go along. I'm guessing we'll be done around one or one-thirty."

"Okay, then. Text me when you're winding up and I'll get things started."

He grinned. "I'll call you."

She rolled her eyes. "I keep forgetting you're stuck in the Stone Age."

Monty swallowed a laugh. His dad used to tease Graham about this. Evidently his mom had taken up the cause.

"It's impersonal."

"Practical."

"My fingers are too big for those itty-bitty keys."

"My boys manage it."

"They're young. More flexible fingers."

"Spence managed it."

"That man could've made the sun stand still if he'd put his mind to it. In case you haven't noticed, I'm not Spence. I'll call you."

She sighed. "And I could be up to my elbows in something or other and can't answer."

"I'll leave you a message. I don't need my fingers for that."

"*Eres muy terco,* Graham Harrison."

"That's what makes me special."

That earned him a chuckle. "See you and Zinnia for lunch."

After his mom left, Monty led the way to the barn for the traditional walk-through. Graham liked to start that way, particularly in the spring when he hadn't seen the horses for almost three months. In the past, Monty's dad had accompanied him.

Now it was Monty's job, and this time the extremely tantalizing Zinnia would be making the rounds with them. He prayed that the familiar routine would override his current attack of lust.

"I've been so curious about this barn." Zinnia paused before the open doors. "My uncle told me your sister and brother-in-law have an apartment in the hayloft." She glanced up at the solid panel that covered what used to be the hayloft doors.

"They sure do. Did Graham tell you about the Beaver Bunch?"

"He did! Those little critters sound awesome. Like something out of Disneyland."

"Exactly what I thought when I first saw them on New Year's Day." Monty latched onto a safe topic. "Cole hits a switch, a platform rotates and out pop three animatronic beavers playing music."

"That must be amazing."

"You know what? We'll be having a party Saturday night and they'll be on display. You should come out. Both of you." Good thing he remembered to add Graham to the invite.

"That sounds like fun. What's the occasion?"

"My birthday, but please don't bring a gift." He hadn't thought of that and certainly didn't want them to feel obligated. "Just yourselves."

"Since my uncle's known you for so long, I'm sure we can come up with an idea." She hesitated. "Would it be okay if I brought Tex?"

Did she have a *husband*? His dreams of using the party as a chance to get to know her better evaporated. "Sure. Is he your—"

"He's my son."

He blinked. She had a *kid*?

"He just turned five. I promise he'll behave himself, but if this is an adults-only party, then...."

"Tex is certainly welcome. By all means bring him. He'll love the Beaver Bunch."

"Thanks." She gave him a warm smile. "He also loves birthday parties."

"Me, too." And he had some thinking to do. He shouldn't be surprised she had a kid. Many of his friends had them and she was a couple years older, around his brother Luis's age. Luis and Jordan were expecting their first baby in July.

Evidently Tex's dad wasn't on the scene. But a five-year-old sure did complicate the picture.

Could be confusing for that little guy, maybe even disruptive.

Because of that she might not be looking for a relationship. Even if she'd consider it, was he up to that kind of challenge? He'd better decide before he issued any more invitations or entertained any more fantasies.

He'd never even contemplated marriage, let alone fatherhood. His body might want her, but his brain told him to take a step back.

2

Another one bites the dust. Zinnia allowed herself a brief sigh of regret. But even if Monty hadn't signaled a switch in his intentions after hearing about Tex, she wouldn't have encouraged him.

She had her priorities straight. No dating until Tex was older. Much older.

But that didn't mean she was immune to the charms of Montgomery Bridger. He was totally her type, physically and mentally.

During the walk-through she absorbed the affectionate tone in his voice as he introduced each of the horses. He'd dedicated his life to taking care of their ailments and she admired the hell out of that choice.

According to her uncle, Monty was a dedicated healer who would sleep in a sick horse's stall if they needed monitoring through the night. He'd drop whatever he was doing to rush to the aid of any horse in trouble. On top of caring for the ones in the barn, he kept tabs on the wild ones that roamed Laughing Creek's vast sanctuary.

He had hero written all over him — kind, generous and easy on the eye. His muscular build and clear blue eyes stirred longings she hadn't satisfied in five years. She couldn't afford the emotional risk.

When her ex had left during the first year of fatherhood, declaring babies were too much trouble, she'd agreed to give up child support in return for sole custody. Thank God her sister had offered to help.

Clearly Monty wanted her, but so did most unattached men and a few of the attached ones. She had the kind of body that inspired randy thoughts and she'd become adept at discouraging unwelcome advances.

She wouldn't have to worry about Monty. He was a gentleman who understood the score. He would curb his attraction and she'd curb hers.

Sure, she'd briefly fantasized going to bed with him, and he'd likely done the same with her. They could have had a lot of fun together. But the possibility that she'd jeopardize her life with Tex wasn't a chance worth taking.

As the three of them neared the back end of the barn, Monty had yet to identify any of the horses as being his personal ride. So she asked him about it.

"I saved mine for last. Meet my buddy Patient."

A deep red sorrel with a flaxen mane and a lightning-shaped blaze poked his head over the last stall door on the left.

"What a beauty." She smiled. "I assume he's super chill."

"He had to be." Monty rubbed the gelding's nose and scratched under his forelock. "I got him right before I enrolled in vet school and I practiced all kinds of procedures on him. I kept calling him *my patient* instead of his name and finally I quit using his name altogether. He became Patient."

"That's funny." She moved closer and stroked the sorrel's silky neck. "How old is he?"

"Ten."

"Only ten? How old was he when you were using him as a teaching tool?"

"Four."

"And he put up with it?"

"You should have seen how tolerant he was," her uncle said. "I'd come out to shoe the horses and Monty would be in the stall with Patient, poking and prodding every part of that poor horse. Patient just stood there quietly and let him do it."

"Amazing."

"Well, I'd give him little treats, a slice of apple or a chunk of carrot."

"Even so."

"I also explained to him that he was furthering my education, and with his help I'd be qualified to help other horses stay healthy." Monty ruffled the sorrel's light-colored mane. "We were partners, right, buddy?"

Patient snorted.

"Damn straight." Monty grinned. "Speaking of partners, I'd better get out of your way so you two can get started. If you don't mind me asking, how are you planning to divvy up the work?"

"I thought I'd steer Zin toward the most cooperative ones for the first visit." Graham gestured toward Patient. "Like this guy, for instance, and Mila's horse Sol. Probably Woody and Buzz. That team of your dad's is so relaxed they fall asleep while they're getting new shoes."

"Yep." Monty chuckled. "I've seen 'em do it."

His soft laughter brushed the tendrils of desire that still lingered, making her shiver. She'd be wise to keep Uncle Graham nearby whenever she was interacting with this cowboy.

"I'm confident she can handle any of them, though." Her uncle gave her a fond glance. "I've seen her in action. She has the touch."

Her chest warmed. "Thank you."

"Your worthless boss didn't know what he had." He turned back to Monty. "The jerk promised to make her a partner and then gave the position to a guy. I'm guessing he's prejudiced against women farriers, but his loss is my gain."

"And ours."

It was a gallant thing to say and darned if it didn't make her face heat. "I appreciate the chance to work on your horses. I won't disappoint you."

"I'm sure you won't."

The warmth in his eyes created squiggles in her stomach. Taking a breath, she focused on her uncle. "Whatcha say Unc? Shall we get moving?"

"We should. Don't want to be late for lunch."

"And I'll vamoose." Monty gave Patient one last pat. "Let me know if you find any issues."

"I always do."

"Then I'm off." He tipped his hat and ambled down the barn aisle.

She'd always been drawn to the loose-hipped, slightly bowlegged stride of a man who spent a good amount of time astride a horse.

"You like him."

She slowly turned to face her uncle's amused expression. "Of course I do. He's very nice."

"I had a feeling you two would hit it off."

Alarm bells went off. "Meaning what?"

"Well…that you two have a lot in common."

"I hope you're not playing Cupid. Because I—"

"Not at all. I just—"

"You know I'm not on the lookout for a guy, right?"

"I do and I understand. But I've known Monty since he was born, which'll be twenty-seven years this Saturday, and you won't find a more—"

"Look, even if I wanted to consider getting involved with him, which I absolutely don't, he's not in the market for a woman with a five-year-old."

"You don't know that."

"I do know that. The second I mentioned Tex, his whole attitude changed."

"Because he's not an idiot who charges into a complicated situation. That's a good thing. But he likes you, too. Sparks were flying."

"Of course they were. You know how men react to me."

"It wasn't one-sided."

"So I'm not immune to a good-looking cowboy. But I've made it this far and I'm not changing a program that's in the best interests of my son."

Her uncle fell silent. Then he sighed and met her gaze. "You're right, Zin. Please forgive an old guy for butting into a situation that's none of his business."

His gentle voice touched a place in her heart that would always hurt. He sounded so much like her dad. "Oh, hey." She gave him a quick hug. "It's not surprising you'd think like that. You love Monty and you love me."

"I love Tex, too. He's a brave little kid."

"And you think he needs a daddy?" She said it softly.

"Guess so."

"He's got you."

"I know, but I'm more like a grandpa."

"So what? He's crazy about you. I couldn't ask for a better role model for him. I honestly didn't realize how much he'd love it here."

"That was my hope, that the move would benefit all three of you."

"It already has. I'll never be able to thank you enough. Marigold says bartending at the Raccoon is way more fun than where she worked in Great Falls."

"I can believe it. The Raccoon is special." He paused, sucked in a breath. "Full disclosure, suggesting this arrangement wasn't exactly selfless. Seems like I needed you guys, too."

"You did?"

"Not long after your Aunt Adele left, Spence died. That was a dark time, and I turned into a grouchy old bear in a cave, nursing my wounds."

"You weren't grouchy."

"Yeah, I was. Ask Raquel, or any of the Bridgers, for that matter. But thanks to you, Mari and Tex...." His chest heaved. "I see things different."

Her throat tightened again. "I love hearing that."

"I love being able to say it. Now let's shoe us some horses before we start blubbering."

3

Monty doubted that Adam and his mom needed his input on whatever they'd planned to discuss. More likely she'd asked him to come up to the house so she could talk to him about Zinnia.

Did she know about Tex? Probably. She'd been about to say something, but they'd arrived and she hadn't finished the sentence.

When he walked through the front door she called to him from the kitchen, his favorite room in the house. He left his hat and jacket on the coat tree in the entry and breathed in the scent of fresh coffee. Yep, she planned to have a chat.

He'd been in middle school when his parents had the brainstorm to wrap the front porch around the side of the house and add more windows to the kitchen. Now they had a view of Mt. Powell from the large trestle table.

His mom sat in her typical spot at the near end of a long bench that offered a great view of the snow-capped peak. She put down her mug and a copy of the *Mustang Valley Messenger.* "Help yourself to coffee if you'd like some."

"I would." He crossed to the counter and took a mug from the cupboard. "Where's Adam?"

"On his way to town. He and Tracy had a meeting with the state highway department guy."

"Is the crew still on schedule for finishing the road?" Adam had worked with the state for months to improve a treacherous road though a mountain pass that linked Mustang Valley and Highway 93 to the west. A safer road would increase tourism and give Adam his first major achievement as mayor.

"So far, so good. Greta's so excited. Business at Books and Buns should really pick up once it's done. Which reminds me, she brought home some sticky buns last night. They're in that container by the stove."

"You don't have to tell me twice." Popping off the lid, he lifted out a sweet-smelling confection that made his stomach growl. "I keep thinking I'll get into town so I can buy stuff from my sis instead of getting it free, but something always comes up."

"Have you decided what kind of cake you want for your birthday? She said you hadn't told her yet."

"I will." He carried his mug and plate to the table and took the chair at the end. When his dad was alive, that was his spot, but now it went to whoever got there first. "What was the thing you wanted my input on?"

"*Perdon, mijo.* I made that up."

"Figured." He took a bite of the sticky bun and hummed with delight. His little sis made the best he'd ever tasted.

"Zinnia has a little boy. He's five."

"Mm-hm." He finished chewing and swallowed.

"She told you?"

"Only after I invited her to my birthday party."

Her eyes widened. "Just her? Not—"

"I invited Graham, too. That's when she mentioned Tex. I said she was welcome to bring him."

"She also has a sister, Marigold."

"Well, damn. My bad. You did say *those girls* when you talked about the family and I plain forgot."

"You can invite her when they come up for lunch."

"I definitely will. Any more people living out at Graham's place I need to know about?" He took another big bite of the sticky bun.

"That's all." She continued to watch him with those wise brown eyes that had a way of pulling confessions out of him.

He finished chewing, swallowed and took a sip of coffee. Then he let out a sigh. "I guess you could tell she made an impression on me."

"Uh-huh."

"But now...."

"Her son is a problem for you?"

"Not a *problem*, exactly." He traced the rim of his mug with one finger before glancing up again. "I'm just not ready for...." Potential scenarios swirled in his head. "So much could go wrong."

"Zinnia probably feels the same. I did when I was a single mom."

"But Dad changed your mind?"

"Ha. He was as scared as I was. We each had three kids to raise. Neither of us wanted a relationship."

"Then how did he end up at that mixer where you guys met?"

"He only went because Tia Kat and his mother begged him to take them so they could have a night of dancing."

"Why were you there?"

"My friend Beth convinced me that we'd just have a fun evening. I missed dancing so much that I agreed but I backed out at the last minute. She guilted me into it by saying I'd promised."

"Obviously I'm glad you both went. I'll bet Greta and Rio are really glad. They wouldn't exist if you hadn't met that night."

"As my mother used to say, *estaba escrito*, it was written."

"If this is written between me and Zinnia, it's clearly meant as a joke."

"You were kind of funny, *mijo.* When you gasped, I almost lost it. I've never seen you react that way to a woman."

"I never have. I wish I'd been better prepared."

"Better prepared or better protected?"

"Maybe both."

She laid a hand on his arm. "I get it. When I danced with your father I felt completely out of control. That's not me."

"Not me, either." He grimaced. "I probably shouldn't have agreed to help with her mare."

"There's no way you would've said no. Speckles is in a strange place and she has to get through her first foaling with an unfamiliar vet. You're the perfect person for that situation."

"That's what I'll concentrate on. Thanks for reminding me of my priorities. The animals come first. They're the most vulnerable."

"Are you going to let Zinnia pay you?"

"No."

"If you want to create some distance, maybe you should let her pay. Doing it as a favor will put her in your debt."

"I hadn't thought of it like that."

"We're paying her and Graham to shoe the horses. Graham likes us, but he's never offered to do it for free."

"True."

"If you charge her for taking care of Speckles, you're keeping the relationship on a professional basis instead of a personal one."

He gazed at her. "You're one smart lady, mamacita."

"Yes, I am."

"I should get going." He drained the last of his coffee. "Luis asked me to check out the mustang he just brought in for training." Pushing back his chair, he stood. "Thanks for helping me get my head on straight."

"De nada."

He started to walk away, then turned back. "I have a question about that mixer. If both of you were determined not to meet anyone, how did you end up dancing with each other?"

She smiled. "He tried to sit out the whole thing but women kept dragging his reluctant ass onto the floor. I was out there a lot, too. I couldn't bear the sad look whenever I'd say no, so I danced with whoever asked. Obviously that wouldn't be him. That intrigued me, especially since he kept glancing my way."

"But you eventually danced together, right?"

"Just once. When they announced the last number, he left his chair, made straight for me, and held out his hand. I took it."

"And that was that."

"Not exactly."

"Wasn't that the start of the courtship?"

She hesitated, then smiled. "The second we were out on the floor, he said *I'm probably going to regret this.* And I shot back *I'm sure I will, too.* We spent the whole dance coming up with reasons we should never see each other again."

"No kidding. Then what?"

"We said goodbye and went our separate ways."

"But something had to—"

"Two weeks later he showed up at my door and asked me to marry him."

"*What*? I thought you met at the dance and then dated for several weeks before he asked you."

"Just because he proposed doesn't mean I accepted. It was several weeks before he asked again and this time I said yes. He was embarrassed to admit he'd proposed on the basis of a single dance, so we left that out of the story. Doesn't matter now."

"How did he know where you lived?"

"Beth secretly tucked my address and phone number in his jacket pocket while we were on the dance floor, just in case. He didn't find it until two weeks later."

"Where is Beth now? We all owe her a lot."

"Sadly, we lost touch. She met somebody that night, too, and they ended up moving to Arizona. We exchanged Christmas cards but then hers stopped coming. People get busy."

"Well, if you should hear from her, let me know. She changed all our lives for the better."

"She did."

"Did you ever regret dancing with Dad? Like when all of us kids were tearing around picking fights with each other?"

"Not for a second. Your father was a gift and I'm grateful every day that he... crossed that dance floor." Her voice quivered on the last part.

"Aw, Mom." He started toward her.

"I'm okay." She held up her hand like a traffic cop and dabbed at her eyes with the other. "Go help Luis with that mustang."

He hesitated. If she needed to cry, he was there for her.

"I mean it. I'll always miss him like the devil, but I'm getting stronger every day." She cleared her throat and blinked her eyes. "Are you coming to lunch?"

"Maybe I'd better not. You could invite the sister. I don't have to do it."

"But if you're here for lunch, you can practice being around her without getting flustered."

"Alrighty then. I'll be here." Lord help him, he was gonna need that practice.

4

Hot and sweaty after five hours of hard but gratifying labor, Zinnia used the sink in the tack room to clean up before lunch. Her uncle had called Raquel about twenty minutes ago to say they'd be up at the house soon.

"Who was the first to put a sink in their tack room, you or Spence Bridger?" She glanced over her shoulder at her uncle, who was scrolling through pictures he'd taken of Banjo, who had a worrisome scab on his heel.

"Spence. But I was the one who thought of adding a mirror."

"It's a nice perk." Peering into it, she took off her cap, finger combed her hair and pulled it back through the cap's opening. Then she backed away to let her uncle use the sink.

Putting away his phone, he washed his hands, splashed water on his face and reached for the towel hanging on a small rack. "The sink was the important part, though. Spence was always dreaming up ways to make things better and more convenient. Like the electronic gates."

"They're snazzy, all right."

"Raquel hated them." He replaced the towel, pulled off his hat and took a comb from his back pocket.

"Really? Why?" She got a kick out of Uncle Graham fussing with his thick white hair, his only sign of male vanity.

"She didn't like the look of those keypad posts." He tucked the comb away before settling the hat back on his head. "Thought they were too modern, like this was some kind of gated community in the suburbs."

"But he put them in against her wishes? That doesn't sound like the guy you've described to me."

"He eventually sweet-talked her into it. The code is her birthday."

"Nice." The more she heard about Spence the more she wished she could have met him.

"Ready to go?"

"Sure am. I'm hungry." She followed him out of the tack room. "Bye-bye, horsies. See you in six weeks."

"Or two days. You can pay 'em a visit when we come out for Monty's party on Saturday."

"That's right, I could." She had mixed emotions about that party now that she knew her uncle had hoped she and Monty would hit it off. Asking for his help with Speckles was the right thing for her horse. A celebration of his birthday was the wrong thing for her sanity. But Tex would love it.

She glanced over at her uncle. "Any ideas about what we can get him?"

"I'll ask Raquel if he has the latest Rance McLintock book. It just came out, so he might not have bought it yet."

"Isn't that the author who wrote *Tequila Shots in the Dark*? M.R. Morrison's son?"

"It is. You've read that one?"

"Sure have. And all of hers, too. Mari and I tried to get to their signing in Apple Grove last year, but we couldn't make it happen."

"I didn't know you and Mari were fans."

"We are, but we don't keep up like we should. I didn't know Rance had another book out. What's this one called?"

"*A Bullet Through the Beer Keg*."

She laughed. "I'd love to meet that guy. I'll bet he's a hoot."

"You're in luck. Once the new road's done, they'll make it over more often."

"Rance and his mom?"

"The whole fam-damnly. Several of them were involved in renovating that purple Victorian outside of town so they could put in the bookstore."

"No kidding. That's a beautiful old house. I haven't made time to pop in, but I want to."

"Spence's Grandma Lucy used to live there. The Bridgers are leasing the space to the McLintocks."

"So they're business partners?"

"And friends, which is why that new book would be a good gift. But he might have it or someone else might have already bought it for him. Hang on. Let me call Raquel. She'll know." He paused and pulled out his phone.

Zinnia grabbed the chance to look around. She'd been focused on Raquel and Monty when they'd driven in — well, mostly Monty. Then she'd been totally absorbed in shoeing those incredible horses. This was her first chance to survey the area.

The main house resembled others where she'd done farrier work—low slung with a long front porch and a couple of chimneys indicating they had at least two wood-burning fireplaces.

The outbuildings were familiar, too. The main barn, which she loved, had a nostalgic hip-roofed silhouette. The other two were more pedestrian, one for the wild horses Luis brought in for training and potential adoption, and the other for ranch machinery. A large pasture and a couple of corrals were also standard for a Montana ranch.

But nothing had prepared her for the rest. To her left, at the far end of the road leading into the ranch, stood an old-fashioned bunkhouse painted an eye-popping fuchsia.

Closer to her on the same side of the road were two almost identical Spanish casitas, complete with arched windows and low walls surrounding a front patio.

A path that wound behind them led to a large building that could be the indoor riding arena her uncle had described.

Facing the main barn again, she studied the house a few yards behind it. She wouldn't call it a casita. Too big for that. More like a small version of a hacienda, which also had a low wall around a front patio.

On a hill behind it perched a Swiss chalet. Of course. Why not? Not far away a cozy cottage right out of a storybook was tucked into the landscape. A few yards to the left a log cabin peeked through the pines.

"Getting a sense of the place?"

She turned back to her uncle. "It's mind-boggling. Did you say Spence built all these houses?"

"And loved doing it. When the kids got old enough, they helped."

"Why so many, and why so varied?"

"It's a long story. Get one of the Bridgers to tell it. They'll do a better job than me."

"Okay, but do you know why the bunkhouse is fuchsia?"

"Because that's where the kids' grandma and three great-aunties live. They call themselves the Dazzling Damsels and that's their dorm."

"Why on earth do they live in a—"

"Like I said, it's a long story best told by one of them." He tucked his phone away and set off for the ranch house.

"All right." She'd ask a Bridger about the house, but not the Bridger who made her pulse dance the cha-cha. "Does Monty already have the new book?"

"No, ma'am. Raquel had planned to buy it for him but she's fine with us doing it, so we're all set for a gift."

"Awesome. Thanks." She wanted to ask which of the dwellings, if any, was Monty's, but that would be a tell. Didn't matter, anyway. She'd never be inside it.

As she climbed the porch steps, the aroma of vegetable soup tickled her nose and the sound of a man's laughter stole her breath. The man didn't have to be Monty. Family members often laughed the same way. But somehow she knew it was him. She loved the happy sound. Wanted to hear it again.

Her uncle rapped on the front door and opened it. "We're here, ready or not."

"Come on in," Raquel's voice came from the same direction as the mouthwatering scent of warm soup. "It's only the four of us, so we're eating in the kitchen."

"That suits me just fine." Uncle Graham left his cap on the coat tree and gestured for her to go through the door to her right.

She walked into the sunniest kitchen she'd ever seen and maybe the only one with a breathtaking view.

"Wow." Her exclamation covered both the broad-shouldered cowboy setting placemats on the long trestle table and the towering majesty of Mt. Powell through the windows at the far end of the kitchen. Cowboys and mountains. What a combo.

He was hatless. A faint crease denting his thick brown hair made him more human, more approachable. Not necessarily a good thing.

He glanced up and smiled. "Since this is your first time here, you get the chair on the end facing the view."

"I'll happily take it, but can I help with anything?"

"We have it under control." Raquel ladled soup into colorful pottery bowls sitting on matching plates.

"Your dishes are beautiful."

"I love them, too. Tia Carmen got them in Mexico." She tucked half a sandwich on either side of the bowl and handed Zinnia the plate. "Here you go."

"Thank you so much. I'm starving."

"I'll bet."

"How'd it go?" Monty pulled back her chair.

"Great." She flicked a glance in his direction as she sat down. "Patient is such a sweetheart."

"Yeah, he is." His breath brushed the side of her face as he neatly slid the chair up to the table.

Awareness fizzed in her stomach. She managed a breathy *thanks.*

He responded with a soft *welcome.*

Oh, yeah, she felt completely welcome. He might not want to want her, but clearly he couldn't help himself. He likely couldn't bluff worth a damn at the poker table, either.

Uncle Graham took the chair on her left. At first she thought Monty would be within knee-bumping distance on the bench to her right. Then he scooted down one place and Raquel took that spot.

Just as well. Playing footsie with the guy, either accidentally or intentionally was not in her best interests.

Once they were all seated, he brought up the birthday party. "Your sister's invited, too. I didn't think to say that when we were down at the barn."

"That's very kind, and I'm sure Marigold would enjoy coming, but she's bartending at the Raccoon and she's got the Saturday night shift."

"She's working at the Raccoon? How does she like it?"

"She loves it. And since she just started last week, I doubt she'd want to ask for a different shift."

"We'll give her more notice for the next party," Raquel said. "It's been many years since I was the new girl in town, but I remember what that feels like. You both are welcome here anytime. And Tex, of course."

Graham flashed her a smile. "How about me?"

"You know you don't need an invitation."

"Don't I?"

"Of course not. You and Spence...." Then she met his gaze. "I see your point, *amigo*. You two used to do things together, but since he...." She trailed off. "You're welcome anytime, too."

"Good to know."

Something in his voice made Zinnia wonder if... nah. She was projecting.

"Tell us about your little guy," Raquel said. "What's he like? What's he into?"

"He's into cowboys, maybe because Mari and I have country music on all the time. He already thinks of himself as a cowboy, which is why he insists we call him Tex."

"That's not his name?"

"Oh, no. His name's Sebastian. But once he settled on being a cowboy, he wanted a cowboy name. He chose Tex."

Raquel beamed at her. "And you didn't fight him on it. I admire that."

"I'm just hoping it's not permanent. He's named after my dad."

"Oh, dear." Raquel glanced over at Uncle Graham. "How are you dealing with the name change?"

"Y'know, he's only five. He never met his grandfather. Even though we've told him stories, it's not enough to make him love the name. I figure when he's older, he might reconsider."

"That's very evolved of you."

"I can relate," Monty said. "I'm not crazy about Montgomery."

Raquel's chin lifted. "It's a good name. It has gravitas."

"That's the trouble, Mom. It's too fancy. I'm glad there's a short version." He turned to Zinnia. "Did your dad have a nickname?"

"Not really." Zinnia couldn't resist looking at him, soaking up the kindness in his gaze. "His friends tried, but nothing stuck, which was fine with him. He liked his name."

"I suppose you could try Seb or Sebby," Raquel said. "Or maybe Bastian or Bas."

"I ran all those by him. He didn't go for any of them. If you look online, you'll also find Seabass."

Monty grimaced. "Let's hope some kid doesn't come up with that one."

"They probably won't since we're in Montana. Anyway, none of the choices sounded cowboy enough, so here we are."

"Then Tex it is," Raquel said. "I can't wait to meet him. He should have a good time, since we're chock-a-block with cowboys around here."

She smiled. "So I've heard." And one of them was seriously testing the limits she'd placed on herself.

Would it make sense for them to talk about it, get the situation out in the open? Her parents had taught her to meet issues head on and not let a problem fester.

He was coming out this afternoon to check Speckles. That might provide an opportunity to speak with him alone. It was the adult way to handle this inconvenient attraction. Yeah, she'd diffuse this bomb and remove the possibility of an explosion.

5

After lunch Monty followed Graham's shiny red truck over to his place. The guy only had a few acres, just enough for a tidy four-bedroom house, a six-stall horse barn, one corral and a small fenced pasture. He lived simply, which made the gleaming pickup stand out against the background of his frugal lifestyle.

That truck wasn't the only thing that signaled a change. His carefully tended patch of grass in the front yard had brightly colored toys scattered all over it.

The vintage red, yellow and blue Big Wheel brought back memories of the one he'd inherited from his big brother Adam. These days they were expensive if you could even find them. But he could picture Graham combing the internet so Tex could ride this beauty.

The collection of trucks and action figures weren't exactly like the ones stored in the ranch house attic for the next generation, but close. The only thing missing was the five-year-old who played with those things. During lunch Zinnia had showed a few pictures on her phone, so he had a general idea of what Sebastian, aka Tex, looked like.

He'd inherited his mother's curly blond hair. His solemn, green-eyed gaze made him look older than five. His happy grin was a heart-melter.

Glancing through the pictures had started Monty's stomach churning. Adam had been close to that age when their dad married Raquel. Monty had been too young to understand what was going on.

Should he ask Adam what his thoughts had been during that time? Not a good idea. Especially since he didn't plan to get involved with Zinnia and her son.

He parked his truck, spattered with days-old mud, next to Graham's spit-shined one. Graham had taken the dirt roads, both the Bridger's and his, at a snail's pace even though the puddles had dried up. Hilarious.

Thinking about Graham's new fastidious behavior took his mind off the impending meeting with Tex. It shouldn't be a fraught moment, but his chest tightened as he climbed out and followed Graham and Zinnia to the porch.

The front door banged open and a blond-headed tornado wearing jeans, boots and a T-shirt barreled down the steps. "Mommy! Uncle G! We maded *brownies*! They're yummy! We—" He screeched to a halt and stared at Monty, his chocolate-rimmed mouth dropping open. "Who's that?"

"Tex, this is Monty." Zinnia's voice took on a special brand of affection mixed with a warning to be mindful.

Monty recognized the tone. His mom had sounded exactly like that this morning when she'd told him she was fine and he needed to give her some space.

"Hello, Mister Monty."

"Hello, Tex." Damn. This kid was way too appealing.

"You knowed my name?"

"Your mom told me."

"When?"

Zinnia put her arm around her son's shoulders. "This morning, when I was at Laughing Creek Ranch helping Uncle G shoe their horses. Monty's a vet and he's going to help us with Speckles."

"Oh." Tex glanced up at her. "He's a cowboy."

"That, too, son."

"Vets are girls."

"Not always. We just happened to have Geraldine in Great Falls. Here we have Monty. Would you please shake his hand?"

"Yes, ma'am." He marched over and stuck out his hand. "Pleased to meetcha."

"I'm pleased to meet you, too." Nudging back his hat, he resisted the urge to drop into a crouch for the handshake. Something told him that wouldn't go over well with this proud little guy.

Instead he reached down and bent his knees the tiniest bit as he grasped the kid's sticky hand and met his solemn gaze. He had guts. And his mother's green eyes.

Tex gave a firm squeeze and let go. "Speckles is gonna have a baby. It's a boy."

"You know that already?" He glanced at Zinnia.

She nodded. “Some people were eager to find that out in advance, so we did the test.”

“I see.”

“Mommy and me used to ride Speckles but we can’t now. We hafta ride Ginger or Fred.”

His use of *we* probably meant he wasn’t allowed to ride solo yet. Instead he rode double on one of Graham’s horses. They were named after a famous old-timey dance team and thanks to Graham, Monty knew all about Ginger Rogers and Fred Astaire.

The little boy’s chest puffed out. “I’m a good rider.”

“I’ll bet you are.”

“I *could* ride all by myself, but nobody lets me.”

“Well, Ginger and Fred are pretty far off the ground.” The kid needed a pony. One like Little Bit, who’d hauled the Bridger kids around for—

“I’m not scared.”

“I believe you.”

“He’s fearless.” Graham said it with pride. “You’re gonna be a super-duper cowboy someday, right, buddy?”

“I sure am, Uncle G!”

“What happened to my helper?” A slender woman several inches shorter than Zinnia walked out on the porch carrying a kid-sized cowboy hat. She shared Zinnia’s classic facial features, but her hair was a darker blonde and didn’t have Zinnia’s wild curls. The red streaks looked like a deliberate addition.

She zeroed in on him. "Oh, hey! I didn't realize we had a visitor. Are you by any chance Monty Bridger?"

"Yes, ma'am." He tipped his hat. "You must be Marigold."

"I am. Thanks for coming by. We've been biting our fingernails to the quick over whether you'd be available. I'm no expert, but I think she's close. Tex and I gave her a fresh bed of straw this morning and decided to keep her in the barn, just in case."

"Good planning."

"This's my Auntie Mari." Tex pointed to her as he accepted the hat she'd brought him. "Want a brownie?"

"I would love one after I take a look at Speckles. Want to come?"

"You bet!" He crammed on the hat.

"We'll all come." Marigold took off her apron and left it on the porch railing. "Everyone has a stake in this birth."

"We're having *steak*?" Tex wheeled to face her. "What about the meatloaf?"

"We're having meatloaf, sweetie. I was talking about a different kind of stake, like the ones we pound into the ground when we anchor the pup tent."

His face scrunched up. "We're putting the tent in the barn?"

Monty choked back a laugh. His little sis Greta used to say things like that when she was Tex's age. He'd forgotten what it was like to have a small child around.

Zinnia walked over and put her arm around her son's shoulders. "We're not doing that, either. It's complicated."

"Sure is." He held out both hands, palms up. "I don't gots a stake, Mommy."

"Yes, you do." She smiled. "It's invisible."

"What?"

"Come on." She gave his shoulders a squeeze and coaxed him toward the barn. "Trust me."

Tex let out a resigned sigh and glanced back at Monty. "She *always* says that."

His breath caught. Something like ten minutes had passed, and Tex was already treating him like a new friend, one who needed an interpreter to explain how things worked around here.

Tex had clearly appointed himself to the job. Whether it had been the Stetson and boots or his skill as a vet, he'd passed muster. He was in.

He wasn't sure what to think about that. But once he entered the barn all his attention snapped to the Appy pacing in her stall.

Her white and black spotted coat was gray with sweat and milk dripped from her swollen udder. She kept glancing back at her belly as if she was telling that little one to get a move on.

He turned to the group assembled next to her stall. Zinnia had picked up Tex so he could see over the stall door.

He gave a little gasp. "She's leaking, Mommy."

"That's milk for her baby." She looked at Monty. "What do you think?"

"She's very close." He glanced at the empty hay net. "You might want to go ahead and feed her. She likely won't eat now, but she'll need it after she gives birth. I'll get my stuff from the truck."

"How close is she?"

"I think tonight." Good thing he'd brought everything he needed, including a cot. He wouldn't be going home anytime soon.

6

Thank God Monty had agreed to come. Speckles needed him. Zinnia transferred Tex to Mari and filled the hay net with the alfalfa mix she'd picked up at the Mustang Valley Feed Store last week.

Her mare showed no interest in the pricey food as she wore a track in the straw, while periodically glancing back at her swollen belly. She wanted that baby out.

Zinnia knew the feeling. She'd had a calm and experienced midwife to help her give birth, but when you've never been through it, the process seemed endless and scary. She remembered—

"Talk about good timing."

Mari's voice pulled her back from that life-changing moment five years ago. "No kidding." She left the stall and latched the door behind her. "When do you have to leave for work?"

"Not for another hour. If she foals soon...."

"She wants to." Tex shifted his weight and Mari adjusted her hold on him.

"Sure looks like she does." Uncle Graham kept his gaze on the Appaloosa. "I don't have a lot of personal experience, but I've heard Monty talk about it. Between that and what we found online, I'd say she's close."

"Yup." He mimicked his great-uncle's expression as he nudged back his hat.

"Exciting, huh?" Mari moved him to her other hip. "Soon we'll know if we have another Appy in the family."

"We will, Auntie Mari."

"Remember, no guarantees."

"I asked Speckles. She nodded her head."

"Works for me." Mari looked outside. "Shouldn't he be back by now? What if he got an emergency call? Do we know if he can even stay?"

"He'll stay."

Zinnia picked up on the warmth in her uncle's voice. "How do you know?"

"The gleam in his eyes. That's how he gets when he's committed to seeing something through. That's why I call him Supervet."

"Good thing you know him so well." She ducked her head to hide a smile. He was still intent on promoting the guy. Doing a decent job of it, too. Who wouldn't be attracted to someone with that kind of dedication?

"I've been keeping an eye on Monty for years. He's turned into a good man."

"Takes one to know one. Hey, Mar, let me hold Tex for a while."

"Nah, it's my turn." Uncle Graham held out his arms. "Come on over, buddy."

Tex wrapped his arms around his great-uncle's neck. "I wish she'd have that baby rrright now."

"We all want that," Zinnia said. "But you know what? You still haven't decided on his name."

"It gots to be a cowboy name."

"I know." Her son was adamant on that point. He disapproved of naming horses after two fancy dancers.

Speaking of Ginger and Fred, maybe they should be brought in and fed early, too. She was about to suggest that when her uncle beat her to the punch.

"Hey, Tex, since it doesn't look like Speckles is going to have that foal in the next twenty minutes, that gives us time to round up the herd. We should do that now, don't you think?"

Her son readily agreed. He might not like the names his great uncle had chosen but he adored those horses. He'd dubbed Speckles, Ginger and Fred *the herd* and pretended they had to be rounded up every night.

As her uncle fetched the lead ropes and left with Tex striding along by his side, Mari turned to her. "Think I should put the meatloaf and baked potatoes in now or wait?"

"Let's start it now. If you put everything in and set the timer, dinner will be done a little early, but at least we won't forget and end up eating peanut butter sandwiches."

"Then I'll go do that."

"You're a sweetie for fixing dinner. It doesn't seem fair that you won't be here to eat it."

"Don't feel sorry for me. Clem's generous with the food for his employees. Listen, if I have to leave before the big event, take pictures and text them to me, okay?"

"Absolutely."

"I'll be right back." She hurried toward the open barn door. "Ah, here comes our hero." She stepped outside and raised her voice. "Monty, just so you know, there will be plenty of meatloaf and I'll throw in another potato for you. There's beer in the fridge for toasting the baby."

"I appreciate that, Marigold. Thanks." He came in hatless, carrying an official-looking metal case in one hand, a folded cot under his arm and a large insulated jug in the other hand.

"Is that coffee?"

"Warm water for cleanup." He set it down along with the case and leaned the cot against the nearest wall. "Where'd Graham and Tex go?"

"They're rounding up the herd." And here they were alone. She'd planned they'd have a discussion once the opportunity presented itself. Although tension crackled in the air, now wasn't the time to deal with it.

"He has cattle stashed somewhere?" He unsnapped his cuffs and started rolling back his sleeves.

"No cattle, just Ginger and Fred." She glanced away and kept babbling. "Normally Speckles would be out there, too." She gestured in that direction while offering an unnecessarily long explanation. "Tex calls it *rounding up the herd* even though the minute he and my uncle show up the horses trot right over, ready to come back to the barn for hay flakes and maybe some other goodies."

"Sounds like Tex likes it here."

"He loves it." She risked looking at him. He'd crouched down to open his case and the motion stretched the faded denim covering his muscular thighs and tight butt. Oh, baby.

Moving closer to the stall, she rested her arms on top of the shoulder-high wall and focused on her horse. Was it possible to make it through this foaling without embarrassing herself?

The jury was still out. She registered the rustle of his clothing, his steady intake and exhale of air. Then a subtle hitch in his breathing sent a shiver up her spine. Was he struggling, too?

Desperate to fill the charged silence, she kept talking. "I thought Tex would miss the kids he went to preschool with. He does, but the excitement of being here overrides the sadness."

"That's good."

"I didn't count on his dedication to the cowboy lifestyle. We lived in suburbia and I had to board Speckles. When Tex found out Uncle Graham had a ranch with a barn and two additional horses, he couldn't wait to move."

"He's never been here before?"

"When I was pregnant with him, Aunt Adele made it clear she didn't like little kids. Or kids, period."

"Lovely."

"Yeah, she wasn't exactly the aunt of my dreams. I guess since they're divorced I don't have to call her my aunt anymore."

"If it makes you feel any better, my family didn't like her, either."

"It does make me feel better. Thanks."

"Mom says she married Graham thinking eventually they'd sell this place and buy a condo on the beach in Florida. When she realized that was never gonna happen, she took off."

"I figured it was something icky like that. He doesn't like to talk about it."

"Can't blame him." Snapping the case closed, he stood. "I'm ready to make friends with Speckles."

"Alrighty." Showtime. Heart racing, she faced him.

He was armed with an orange roll of tail wrap, his jug of warm water, a couple of thin towels tossed over one shoulder and scissors tucked in his pocket.

Nothing about that should stir her up. But damn, he looked good standing there. "What can I do?"

"Since she doesn't know me, it'll help if you'll make the introductions."

"Happy to." Lifting her chin, she bravely met his friendly blue gaze. See? They could keep it casual. They….*whoa.* In a flash, warmth morphed into searing heat. She sucked in a breath.

So did he.

The moment stretched and curled around them. She gulped. "Listen, I—"

He broke eye contact and his chest heaved. Clearing his throat, he focused on a point over her shoulder. "Sorry. My fault."

His emotion-roughened voice set her body on fire. "Mine, too."

He swallowed. "We'll talk."

"Right."

"Later."

"Right." Light-headed from lack of oxygen, she fumbled with the latch and finally managed to slide the stall door open. As he followed her in, his nearness made her quiver with longing.

"I won't start the tail wrap until I'm sure she's accepted me."

His matter-of-fact words came out in a husky delivery that conjured up an image of cool sheets and warm bodies. "Okay."

"Once she seems fine with me being there, if you'll keep loving on her from the front I'll take care of things in the back."

"Sounds like a plan." Lord help her. She was a sucker for a tender-hearted cowboy. Clearly Monty was a card-carrying member of that brotherhood.

Speckles had been lying down, but she lumbered to her feet and came over, a clear plea for assistance in her eyes. True to her breed, her eyes had a white ring surrounding the brown iris, giving her a human-like gaze. That was one of many reasons Zinnia had fallen in love with her.

"Hey, Specks." She rubbed the mare's nose and cheeks. "This is Monty. He's a friend and he's going to help you bring your baby into the world."

"Hi, Speckles." Setting down the jug, he held out his hand palm down so she could sniff it. She took her time before lifting her head to study him. He ran his knuckles lightly along her cheek. "This is your show, ma'am, but I'll assist wherever I can." Sliding his hand up to her sweaty neck, he scratched lightly under her mane. "I need to wrap your tail so it won't get in the way. I'll also do a little bit of cleanup to get ready for—"

"Mommy! We—"

A soft murmur from Uncle Graham ended whatever Tex had been about to say.

As the steady thud of hooves on the barn floor grew closer, her son switched to a stage whisper. "*We hafta tell her what we thinked up.*"

"We will, buddy." Her uncle kept his voice low. "But quietly. After we feed these two."

When Fred, a handsome bay, and Ginger, a good-looking roan, passed by the stall, Speckles nickered. Her stablemates responded.

Monty smiled. "She's glad to see them."

"She is. It didn't occur to me she might be comforted by having them in the barn. Looks like we have us a herd, after all."

"Sure does. Feeling more relaxed, Speckles?"

The mare let out a loud sigh that sounded more like a groan.

"I'll take that as a qualified yes. I'll get to work on your tail." Picking up the jug, he moved around to the mare's rump. Speckles swung her head around, watching him until he started wrapping her tail. After another sigh of resignation, she nudged Zinnia, clearly asking for more nose rubs.

She snapped out of her Monty-created daze. The guy even smelled good. That fact hadn't registered until he'd walked away and she suddenly missed that tantalizing combo of soap, leather and a faint hint of spicy aftershave.

"The horses must have bonded pretty fast," Monty said. "How long have you been here?"

"Only two weeks. We crossed our fingers and hoped that Speckles would fit in. You never know. But she did." Her mare was much calmer now. Whether it was a result of her renewed caresses, the presence of the other horses, or Monty's ability to inspire trust, Speckles wasn't frightened anymore.

Zinnia leaned to her left to check Monty's progress on the tail wrap. "You're fast."

He chuckled. "Patient got his tail wrapped a lot."

"No wonder he was so easy to shoe. There's not a problem horse in that barn, but Patient is by far the most cooperative. I told him so, too."

"I'm sure he liked hearing that."

On top of everything, the guy had a nice voice. His relaxed delivery in a normal conversation like this was seductively easy listening. But his husky tone from a few minutes ago had created scenarios that made her blush. Good thing nobody could read her mind, although he might have been able to in the moment. She'd certainly read his. Eventually they'd talk and set some—

"We feeded Ginger and Fred." Tex's announcement and the tap-tap of his boots preceded him. He appeared in the open stall door holding an old wooden stool about two feet tall. "Whatcha doing to her tail?"

Monty gave him a quick glance. "I need to wrap it so it won't get in the way. Her baby will come out the back."

Tex's eyes widened. "How?"

"This area here will stretch out."

"How big?"

"Big enough for her foal to come out." He snipped off the end of the roll and finished up.

"Then what?"

"Once he's out, she'll close up again."

"Are you sure?"

"Yes."

Tex let out a breath. "That's a relief."

"Nature's amazing. Hey, sport, if I toss this out to you, would you please put it on top of my case?"

"Yes, sir!" He put down his stool. "I gots a stool."

"I see that. Okay, coming atcha." He lobbed the tail wrap out the door. It plopped against Tex's chest and he managed to grab it before it fell.

"Got it!" He held it aloft.

"Great catch."

He grinned. "I know." He started to leave.

"Thank you."

"You're welcome." He was still grinning as he left.

Zinnia told herself not to get misty-eyed over the interaction, but damn, why couldn't her worthless ex have been a nice guy like Monty?

Soon Tex came back, picked up his stool and glanced at her. "Uncle G let me have this so I can see over the wall."

She nodded. "Smart move."

"I can't be in there. Uncle G won't be in there, either."

"It might be best if nobody's in here." Monty dampened a towel and started gently washing Speckles' hindquarters. "At least in the beginning. I might need to give her a little assistance, but she'll mostly handle it on her own."

Tex studied the process. "She will. She's a good horse." Then his attention shifted. "Mommy, me and Uncle G thinked up a name."

"Oh, you did, did you?" Thank heavens he'd finally settled on something after weeks of discussion. "That's great. What is it?"

"It's a really good one."

"I'm sure it is if you like it."

"I do. I like it a lot."

"So? What is it?"

He flashed her a grin. "Monty."

7

Monty almost dropped the towel. "You want to use my name?"

"Yup."

"I'm honored, sport, but there are so many other great names. How about Levi, or Ranger, or hey, Domino might be great for an Appy. Or Chief, since these horses were bred by the Nez Perce."

"I like Monty."

He didn't know what to say. The kid had caught him flat-footed. He'd love to know how Zinnia felt about this turn of events. He'd been so stunned he hadn't thought to check her reaction.

He did that now, and she looked unfazed. He didn't believe that for a minute. She'd clearly had time to compose herself.

"Fred and Ginger are settled in." Graham appeared in the doorway to the stall. "How's everything going?"

"Just dandy. Tex has informed us of the name you two picked out." He studied the guy's expression and took note of the twinkle in his eyes.

Graham held up both hands, palms out. "It was Tex's idea. He started asking questions about you, so I gave him a little background, told him about Laughing Creek Ranch and the Bridger

Bunch. At the end of that, he announced his decision."

"It's a cowboy name." Tex picked up his stool and disappeared. Then he popped up over the wall from his new perch. "For a cowboy's horse."

"What's this I hear?" Marigold walked into the barn bringing the distinctive aroma of brownies. She came over to stand next to Tex's stool. "You've finally settled on a name for your horse?"

"A *great* name. Monty. You bringed us brownies?"

"I did. Are you naming your horse after our new friend here?" Her voice quivered as if she might be trying not to laugh.

"Yup."

"Catchy."

Evidently nobody was willing to talk the little guy out of his choice. Sounded like it had been a long road to get to this point and the happy smile on Tex's cherubic face was touching as hell. Time to accept this gracefully and hope the kid changed his mind later.

He sucked in a breath. "I think it's very cool. I've never had anybody named after me. Thanks, Tex."

"You're welcome. Want a brownie?"

"Sounds awesome." He glanced toward Zinnia. "Let's go eat brownies and give Speckles some room to roam."

"I'm in." She placed a kiss on her mare's nose. "I'll be close by, pretty girl."

Picking up his jug, Monty followed her out of the stall.

As he put it down next to his case, Marigold caught his gaze. "Any thoughts on when it will happen?"

"Likely in the next few hours, but I can't pinpoint it any better than that. At least we got her tail wrapped. Now we wait."

"Can I pass out brownies?" Tex slid off his stool and reached for the container.

"Only after you wash up, buddy." Marigold lifted it out of reach.

"That goes for the rest of us, too," Graham said. "You guys go ahead. I'll fetch a couple of hay bales so we can sit."

"I'll help." Monty tucked away the scissors and tail wrap before catching up with Graham as he headed toward the rear of the barn.

When they were far enough from Marigold, who'd perched on Tex's stool to wait, Graham lowered his voice. "Sorry about the name thing. I can tell it threw you."

"A little."

"I tried to convince him it'll be confusing, but he said it wouldn't be since you're *Mister* Monty and his horse will be just Monty."

"And it's always possible he'll change his mind."

"Wish I could agree with that. But he's a stubborn little cuss. Once he grabs onto something, he holds on for dear life."

"You mean like renaming himself Tex?"

"Exactly." Graham met his gaze. "Reminds me of you at that age, hell-bent on being called Monty."

"But I didn't change the whole thing. I only shortened the one I had."

"Your dad kept using Montgomery, though."

"Talk about stubborn. At first I was mad, but then I let it go."

"He didn't tell you why he was doing that?"

"No. Thought about asking. Never did." Something in Graham's expression made his gut clench. "Do I want to know?"

"Um...."

"Am I named after someone special, like Tex, and nobody told me?"

"Nothing like that." He frowned. "Doggone it. Shouldn't have brought it up. I figured he'd told you."

"Well, now you've gotta tell me. You can't just leave me hanging."

"Guess not." He sucked in a breath. "Emily loved the name, started using it the minute the doc said she'd have a boy. She predicted you'd end up with a nickname, but she'd still call you Montgomery. Your dad used it to honor her memory."

Because she'd died giving birth to him. Graham's words bounced around in his chest, eventually gathering into a tight ball of anger. He'd learned how and when she'd died when he was seven, old enough to ask for details.

He'd gone to Raquel, the only mother he'd ever known, curious about the pretty blonde woman in the picture he'd been given many years before. He'd instinctively trusted her with his questions. In answering them, she'd soothed his distress and relieved his natural but misplaced guilt.

But she hadn't told him this, likely because she'd rightly decided it was up to his dad. Had she urged her husband to explain himself to his son? Probably. "He should—" He paused to take a breath. "He should've told me."

"Probably couldn't figure out how. Especially after time went by."

Graham's gentle tone helped, but damn it! All those years.... "I suppose." Staring at his fists, he slowly unclenched them.

"Listen, I didn't mean to—"

"It's okay." Monty squeezed Graham's shoulder. "I'm glad you told me." Not ready to meet the guy's sympathetic gaze, he glanced down the aisle. "Zinnia and Tex are coming out of the tack room. We'd better get a move on."

"Yessir." Graham grabbed the top hay bale.

"Maybe I should start using it."

"Don't know if I could make the switch." He swung the bale to his shoulder. "Want me to try?"

He sighed and shook his head. "It's been too long." He grabbed a hay bale. "I sure hope Zinnia explains things to Tex before it's too late." And why was he worrying about something that was none of his damn business?

"Your story would probably help make that point." Graham turned and headed down the aisle.

Hoisting the bale to his shoulder, he followed. "Feel free to tell her."

"Not mine to tell."

The irony of that wasn't lost on him. He was his father's son when it came to emotional conversations. On top of that, sharing a piece of his personal history with Zinnia would draw them closer together, something he'd been planning to avoid.

He considered his options as he walked toward the little group, people he'd only met today. Three strangers, really.

Except he'd done a lousy job of maintaining his distance from that spunky crew. Zinnia and Marigold were amazingly resilient considering they'd lost both parents and it looked like Tex's dad had flown the coop.

Even if he took his mom's advice and accepted payment for monitoring the birth of Speckles' foal, that transaction wouldn't do the trick. This situation was already more than a job.

Big surprise, he'd become invested in helping to create good outcomes for everyone, especially Zinnia. So far he'd been able to keep his libido in check, though.

Having Tex around made that easier by reminding him a kid was a huge responsibility—one he wasn't looking for.

8

Tex babbled non-stop about his new friend while Zinnia helped him wash up. Uncle Graham must have spilled the beans about the birthday party while he'd been describing Laughing Creek Ranch and the Bridger Bunch. Tex had a thousand questions about that, none of which she could answer.

Her son had forgiven her ignorance with a quick *it's okay, I'll ask Mister Monty.* Her son had interacted with plenty of adults in his short life and had liked many of them. But he'd never developed a crush.

His adoration promised to make her avoidance plan a challenge, especially because she agreed with him on the excellence of Monty Bridger. She understood why Tex wanted to name his foal after that cowboy and refused to consider the confusion that might result.

Not that she'd ever mix up the two. As he came toward her balancing a hay bale on his shoulder, her heartbeat shifted into double-time. She'd asked the Universe for a kind and capable vet for her mare. The Universe had overdelivered.

Tex popped the lid off the glass container of brownies and picked up the tongs tucked inside.

"Better wash up fast, Mister Monty if you want brownies."

"I do and I will." He set the hay bale next to Tex's stool. "Have a seat, ladies."

"Thanks." Zinnia gave him her standard *we're just friends* smile. After taking another peek at Speckles, who was back to pacing the stall, she settled onto the crunchy surface of the hay bale.

"He likes you," her sister murmured, plopping down beside her.

"Mm."

"You like him, too."

"*I* like him." Tex perched on his stool, hat nudged back and his boot heels hooked over the wooden rung below his seat, looking for all the world like a miniature cowboy at a bar except for the brownies in his lap. "I like him a *lot.* He gots a birthday, Auntie Mari, and we're going."

"We are?" Her brows shot up.

"It's this Saturday night, sis. I'm guessing that switching shifts is a non-starter, but if you—"

"Yeah, too soon, but a birthday party sounds like fun. I'd like to meet that family."

"Monty's mother Raquel said we're welcome anytime."

"That's nice of her. Was she the one who invited you to the birthday party?"

"Uh, no. That was Monty."

"I see." Mari gave her a knowing glance.

She lowered her voice. "It's not what you're thinking."

"Zin, maybe it's time for—"

"Here he comes." Excitement rippled through Tex's announcement, as if a celebrity had just emerged on stage.

She had the same reaction, but she stuffed it. Not much she could do about her son, though.

He gazed at Monty, hero worship shining in his eyes. "Do ya want a brownie, now?"

"I'd love one. But first I'd better check on Speckles. Be right back." Walking over to the closed stall door, he shoved his hands in his pockets and focused on the mare's steady progress around the stall.

"I'll take one, please." Zinnia got a napkin from Mari and held out her hand, the napkin laid across her palm. They'd practiced this routine many times. He loved passing out baked goods.

He shook his head and dropped his voice to a reverent whisper. "We should wait."

She chuckled. "Okay."

"Have a napkin, Uncle Graham, so you're ready." Mari handed one over. He'd taken a seat on the hay bale next to her. "If we don't start eating them soon I'll have to skip it."

"Hey, I'm sorry." Monty turned and came toward them. "I thought you'd all just go ahead."

"It seems you're the man of the hour." Mari held out a napkin. "You're supposed to go first."

"Ah." He took the napkin. "May I please have a brownie, Tex?"

"You gots to put the napkin on your hand and hold it out."

"Like this?"

"Perfect." The tip of his tongue poked out as he manipulated the tongs with the concentration of a brain surgeon. The brownie ended up in the exact center of the napkin.

"Nicely done."

A proud grin lit up his face. "Thanks."

Zinnia's insides turned to mush. But she dared not get used to this kind of interaction. It wasn't like Monty would be hanging around after this episode with Speckles ended.

While Tex passed out the brownies, Monty gave his report between bites. "I still think it'll be tonight. Wish I could be more specific, but I can't." He polished off his brownie. "Delicious."

"Auntie Mari and me, we maded them." Tex gazed at the ones left in the pan, his lips moving. "Five!" His focus shifted to the people. "One, two, three, four. We gots an extra, Mommy."

"I think that's for you, sweetie."

"Oh." He giggled. "I'm five." Holding up his hand, he stretched out his fingers and thumb toward Monty. "Guess how old I am."

"Five?"

"Rrright!"

"Hey there, Tex." Mari held out her napkin. "Can I please have my second one? My time's running short."

"Yes, ma'am." He carefully transferred the brownie before turning back to Monty. "Auntie Mari can't come to your party. Maybe we can save her some cake."

"Absolutely. I'll make sure you get a slice to take home." He glanced at Mari. "Sorry you can't make it."

"So am I." She smiled. "Uncle Graham thinks a lot of your family. So does my boss Clem. I'm eager to meet them all."

"We'll make that happen real soon."

"Excellent."

"Want your other brownie, Mister Monty?"

"I do. Thanks."

"You're welcome. Uncle G says you gots a big herd."

"My family does."

"My family gots a little herd."

"Size doesn't matter, sport."

"Sometimes it does. Right, Zin?" Mari sent her a bright smile.

"I have no idea what you're talking about." She narrowed her eyes at her unhelpful sister. "Isn't it about time for you to get ready for work?"

"Afraid so." She popped the last of her brownie into her mouth and stood.

"I'll come with you. I want to stick a fork in the potatoes and see how they're doing." She left her napkin on the hay bale and followed Mari.

"They won't be done yet."

"No harm in checking." The minute they were outside she lowered her voice. "What are you up to?"

"Building a fire under your butt. He's amazing."

"So what? I'm not interes—"

"Tell that to someone who doesn't know you."

She ducked her head and kept her voice to a murmur. "Okay, I like him, but it's pointless."

"Oh, there's a point. Have you seen how he looks at you?"

Heat flooded through her. "That's nothing new. Guys are always—"

"But this one comes with Uncle Graham's stamp of—"

"I know, and I've already told our dear uncle to back off. Now I'm telling you."

"Then you'd better tell Monty, because unless he's blind, he knows you're into him."

"And we'll have that discussion the minute I get the opportunity. I can't risk upsetting Tex's—"

"That's the other thing. He's nuts about Monty. It's adorable." Mari quickened her pace and bounded up the porch steps.

"Which is even more reason to put the skids on this." Zinnia followed her into the house. "Monty doesn't want to take on a woman with a kid."

"How the hell do you know that?" Toeing off her battered ranch boots, she started toward her bedroom.

"I saw his face this morning when he found out I have a five-year-old. It freaked him out."

Mari paused at her door and turned around. "Well, he isn't freaked out now. Just the opposite. He's been very sweet to Tex."

"He's a nice guy. But just because he's kind to my son doesn't mean he'd be fine taking on that kind of responsibility. He's only twenty-seven, Mar."

She clapped a hand to her chest. "You cradle robber, you!"

"Cut it out. I'm just saying—"

"You're just saying you're scared spitless because after years of rebuffing every man who takes an interest, you've crossed paths with one who blows all the others out of the water. And you want him."

"I can't let myself get carried away. I have to think of Tex."

"I know you do. And maybe Monty's too young, and too freaked out about Tex, but from my perspective, he has the makings of a dream come true. You might need to give him some time, but—"

"Too risky."

Mari gazed at her. "It's already risky. Tex has a serious crush."

"I know." Her chest tightened. "I can't decide what to do about that."

"How about asking Monty how he wants to handle it?"

"Oh." The concept sent fizzy bubbles dancing in her stomach.

"Listen, I have to hit the showers or I'll be late."

"I know. I'll go check the potatoes." She headed for the kitchen.

"Like it or not," Mari called after her, "you and Monty are in this together."

Her breath caught. They were. And she didn't hate the idea. Which was another red flag.

9

Monty remained standing so he could keep an eye on Speckles while he finished his second brownie. Graham kept his spot on the hay bale he'd brought from the back and Tex continued to occupy the battered old stool.

After cleaning the last crumbs out of the brownie pan, Tex pointed to himself, Monty and Graham. "One, two, three. Three cowboys."

Graham nodded. "That's a fact, kiddo."

"I know." His gaze swung toward Monty. "Do you gots a daddy?"

The unexpected question sent a jolt of emotion through his heart. "Yes. I mean, I did. He died."

"When?"

"Two years ago." Time was a funny thing. It could stretch, shrouding a past event in mist, or compress and throw it into sharp focus, like now. Maybe Graham's presence had something to do with it, jumpstarting memories of the two friends cracking jokes, even in the dark times. Especially the dark times.

"Was he a cowboy?"

"He was. Best ever."

"That's the God's truth." Graham sounded like he had a head cold.

"I gots a daddy. He's not here."

"I noticed."

"Mommy says he *wants* to be my daddy, but he's not up to it."

"That's unfortunate." He snuck a peek at Graham, whose jaw had turned to stone.

"It's okay." Tex shrugged. "He's not a cowboy."

"That's for sure." Graham's scowl indicated he had more to say on the subject, but clearly Zinnia had taken the high road when explaining her ex's absence to her son.

"Do you gots a mommy?"

"I do." Might as well not get into the details of that. "She's looking forward to meeting you at the birthday party."

"How many days do I gots to wait?"

"Two."

"I wish it was tomorrow."

"You'll want to be here tomorrow so you can start making friends with your foal." He couldn't bring himself to use his name for that colt.

"Speaking of birthdays," Graham said, "Looks like today will be someone's birthday."

"Whose?"

Adorable. He really hadn't figured it out.

"Your horse!" Graham chuckled as the light dawned on that innocent little face.

"Oh! My *horse*!"

"If he's born before midnight, today will be his birthday."

Looked like Graham wasn't eager to use the name Monty, either.

"You mean *Monty's* birthday." Then he giggled. "Then comes *Mister* Monty's birthday. Twins!" He glanced toward the barn door as Zinnia walked through it. "Mommy, I gots something to tell you."

"What's that, sweetie?" Zinnia had left her cap in the house. Looked like she'd brushed her hair, too. It fell in golden waves to her shoulders.

That probably wasn't a signal that she wanted him to slide his fingers through it. But he sure wanted to. Oh, hey... was she wearing lipstick?

What was that supposed to mean? She hadn't worn it this morning, so why now? In any case, he needed to stop staring at her tempting mouth ASAP.

"Guess what?" Tex wiggled on the seat, clearly excited about his news.

She grinned. "What?"

"Monty and Mister Monty almost have the same birthday. Isn't that funny?"

"Yes. Yes, it is." She pressed her lips together as if holding back a laugh. Then she swallowed and turned in his direction. "What do you think, Mister Monty?"

"It's funny, all right." He held her gaze. Definitely lipstick. "How're the potatoes doing?"

She took a second to answer, as if she had trouble processing the question. Then she blushed and shifted into efficiency mode. "They're almost done." She glanced at her uncle. "Would you and Tex please go make a salad? I need to discuss a few things with Monty."

"We're on it." Graham stood and reached for the brownie pan in Tex's lap. "C'mon, cowboy. Let's rustle up some grub."

"But I don't wanna miss—"

"I'll call Uncle G if Speckles goes into labor." Zinnia held up her phone. "I'll make sure you don't miss anything. I need you to help with the salad. Will you do that, please?"

"Yes, ma'am." Tex got to his knees and peered into the stall. "It's okay, girl. I'll be right back."

The mare gave a snort.

"She's gonna wait for me." He slid off the stool and started out of the barn with Graham. "Can I use the sharp knife, Uncle G?"

"If you promise to take it super slow, buddy."

"I promise."

The minute they'd cleared the open doorway, Monty's heart began misbehaving. He couldn't breathe worth a damn, either.

She turned to him, her color high, her voice seductively low. "This is about Tex."

"Is it?"

"He's decided you're his new hero."

"You put on lipstick."

"Yes, I did." Her breathing was wonky, too.

He stepped closer, breathed in her citrus scent. "Why?"

"It's the kind that smears."

"You think I'd grab you? I'd never—"

"You're not the one I'm worried about."

"Oh." That info ramped him up even more. Too bad he'd just declared that he'd never grab her. He shoved his hands in his pockets. "So."

"So." She copied his move and put her hands in her pockets. But instead of meeting his gaze, she focused on a point over his right shoulder. "As I was saying, Tex has serious hero worship."

"No kidding. Any chance you can talk him out of naming this foal after me?" He couldn't seem to stop looking at her mouth. And the pale pink lipstick she'd applied to keep herself from kissing him.

"I hope so. But not today. This foal is a big deal for him."

"I get that." She had the perfect mouth for kissing—a cupid's bow on top and a plump lower lip that was just begging to be nibbled.

"He'll probably remember it forever."

The kid likely wasn't the only one. Standing close to a woman he wanted to kiss, a woman who'd indicated she was similarly inclined, and being stymied by her recently applied lipstick....

"Like I said, Tex wants to be like you."

"True." That lipstick wouldn't last forever. The kind that smeared never did. By the time they finished dinner, it would be gone.

"Mari and I talked about it. She suggested I ask you how you wanted to handle it."

"Me? He's your kid. I have zero experience with something like this." But when it came to kissing, he had enough experience to know how sweet those lips would be, how supple, how—

"You've never had somebody's little kid take a shine to you?"

"Can't say that I have. But I'll bet this isn't the first time Tex has latched onto a random adult."

"Actually, it is." She finally looked at him. "His social life in Great Falls consisted of the kids at his pre-school and their parents. None of the dads were cowboys."

"Do you think that's all it is? The outfit?"

"It's the outfit, but it's also your job. You take care of horses. And there's your ranch, and your, um—" She licked her lips and gestured toward him. "Your mannerisms."

Her lower lip glistened where she'd run her tongue over it. He sucked in air. "I don't have mannerisms."

"It's your walk, the way you stand, the tilt of your hat, the tone of your voice…." She trailed off, her gaze locked with his.

His heartbeat was out of control. "Are we…" He paused to clear his throat. "Are we still talking about your kid?"

"Yes. No." She dragged in a breath. "Look, you don't want to get tangled up with me."

"You're right, I don't."

"See, I knew that. You're not ready for—"

"I'm not. But—"

"Then we're on the same page."

"Meaning we want each other?"

"Meaning it's a terrible idea."

"Probably, but—" A groan from the stall grabbed his attention. Turning, he glanced over at Speckles. "Call Graham. It's happening."

10

Zinnia yanked her phone from her back pocket and tapped the screen as she spun around toward the stall. "Graham, she's in labor."

"On our way."

Disconnecting, she moved in beside Monty. Speckles lay on her side, her back to them, her flanks heaving. The straw under her rump was soaked. "Her water broke."

"Yep. I heard it right after she groaned." His breath caught. "And here he comes. There's a hoof. Both hooves. Attagirl. Keep push—"

"Mommy, Mommy!" Tex barreled through the door, his face pink and his eyes wide.

"Shh." She held out her arms to catch him as he raced toward her. "We have to be quiet."

"*Okay.*" His stage whisper wasn't quiet, but it would have to do.

Standing him on the stool, she wrapped an arm around his waist to steady him. He was quivering. So was she, buffeted by aftershocks from that heated conversation with Monty. And now this, a new life joining her little band of survivors.

Graham took Tex's other side, placing a hand on his shoulder. "This is it, buddy. What we've been waiting for."

He murmured a soft "I know," then let out a gasp. "What's that?" He pointed to the translucent, blue-tinted membrane covering the foal's emerging muzzle and forelegs.

"It's called the amnion," Monty said. "He's been living inside it all this time while he grew."

"Can he get out of it?"

"He will, once she pushes him all the way out."

He nodded, his attention glued to the drama in front of him. "She's trying to, but he's stuck."

"She'll get there, sport. She just has to work a little harder to get his shoulders through. And here we go!"

"He's out! Mommy, he's out!"

"He sure is." She gulped and swiped at her eyes, awash in relief and gratitude.

"Will you look at that." Her uncle's gruff voice gave him away.

Tex didn't move, clearly stunned by what he'd just seen.

No wonder. A perfect foal lay in the straw, rubbing his black nose against his leg to get rid of the amnion. Speckles lumbered to her feet and came over to help him, licking and nuzzling her baby.

What a miracle. Zinnia had questioned her decision so many times in the past few months. Had breeding Speckles been a good idea or a foolish waste of money? Was all the effort worth it?

Oh, yeah, so worth it. All she had to do was look at her son's face. As the shock wore off, he was still speechless, but his smile radiated pure joy.

She blinked away fresh tears. He'd missed out on having a daddy, but growing up with a foal that would become his best friend would help balance the scales.

She glanced at Monty and caught him wiping his eyes with a bandanna. And didn't that just tug at her heart, too?

He gave her a sheepish grin. "Gets me every time."

"I can see why. Thank you. Thank you so much."

He shrugged. "Speckles gets all the credit. I just watched."

"But you were here. That meant the world to me, knowing that I didn't have to worry if something didn't go the way it—"

"*Mommy, look.*" Tex pulled on her sleeve. "Monty gots *spots.*"

"Oh, my gosh, you're right!" The foal's dark muzzle was the only solid black on his body. The rest of his coat was decorated with irregular black spots just like his mother's. Speckles had given birth to a beautiful leopard Appy.

"He's already trying to get up, the little bugger." Uncle Graham chuckled as he took his phone from his back pocket. "Guess I'd better record some of this."

Startled, Zinnia looked at the phone in her left hand. "I blew it. I promised Mari pictures of the birth and I totally forgot." She let go of Tex and began videoing the foal's struggle to get his spindly legs under him. "I feel terrible. Now she won't get to see—"

"No worries." Monty's soft voice tickled her sensitized nerve endings. "I got it."

"You took pictures?"

"A video. I'll send it to you."

She sighed in relief. "Thanks for saving my butt. She would have forgiven me, but I probably wouldn't have forgiven myself. I'm so glad you took it."

"I usually do unless I'm assisting with the birth. If I'm filming, I can zoom in and check on the progress while still leaving the mare to handle things on her own."

"Good idea." What a dedicated professional. She admired that. She also admired his ass. What a mess she was, lusting after a man who'd admitted he wasn't ready for the only deal she could offer.

"Come on, Monty!" Tex leaned against the stall, intent on the foal's struggle. "You can do it! I know you can! Go, Monty, go!"

She snuck a glance to check out how the other Monty was taking this. He watched with a bemused expression as Tex continued to use his name to cheer on the foal.

She edged closer to him and lowered her voice. "You hate this, right?"

"I wouldn't say that. But I've never met another person with my name. This is a small town. Whenever someone calls out Monty, I know they mean me."

"That'll still be true unless you're over here."

"Are you saying you're not on board with *Mister* Monty?"

"Only when I'm talking to my son, to avoid confusion. I sure as heck won't be addressing you that way."

His cheek creased in a tight smile. "I appreciate that."

"I suppose I could call you Bridger, though. How would you feel about that?"

"It wouldn't work in a crowd. There's a passel of us."

"I see your point. Maybe you'll be able to tell in context whether I mean you or the foal. Or by my tone of voice."

He grinned. "You'll have a special way of saying my name? That could be interesting."

"Never mind. Bad idea."

"What about Montgomery?"

"I thought you didn't like it."

"It beats *hey, you.*"

"Would you really be okay with me using it?"

"I like it better than trying to guess if you mean me or the foal."

"Then Montgomery it is." She paused the video. "He's still not upright. No telling what's happening with our dinner. Could this be another hour or two?"

"The way he's going, it might only be five minutes."

"Really?"

"They normally don't take long to do it. It's instinctive since they have to stand to be able to nurse."

"Is he ahead of the curve?"

He laughed. "Oh, he's definitely ahead of the curve. After all, he's my namesake."

"But you're not going to call him by it, are you?"

"Not if I can help it."

"Then you probably shouldn't spend much time over here."

"Would you prefer that?"

She met his gaze. "It would be for the best."

"Doesn't answer my question." He had that gleam in his eyes again, the one that turned her brain into a bowl of spaghetti.

She sucked in a breath. "You probably shouldn't look at me that way, Montgomery."

"Your lipstick's gone."

She automatically touched her mouth.

"Then again, I doubt you'd grab me in the middle of this family-friendly event."

"Exactly. I'll put on more as soon as—"

"You did it! You did it, Monty!"

She glanced at the foal, shaky but upright, balanced precariously on those toothpick-thin legs. He took a step, then another, and another. Eventually he reached his mother, dipped his head under her belly and began to nurse.

Belatedly she remembered the phone in her hand. She'd missed the moment once again. "Doggone it! I didn't get the grand finale, either."

"I got it!" Uncle Graham held up his phone. "Hey, who's hungry?"

"Me!" Then Tex looked over at the foal. "But I don't want to leave Monty."

"Tell you what." Uncle Graham tucked his phone away. "You guys stay here and take more pictures while I bring out a card table and the food. We'll eat in the barn. How does that sound to everyone?"

She nodded. "I'm for it. How about you, Montgomery?"

"I'm in. I like picnics."

Uncle Graham gave them each a funny look.

"Mommy, you called him the wrong name."

"That's his full name. Monty is short for Montgomery."

"Mont*gomery* doesn't sound like a cowboy."

"But he still is a cowboy, right?"

His face scrunched up. "Yeah, but...."

Clearly she'd confused him. "How about this. You keep calling him Mister Monty because that's the name you like and I'll keep calling him Montgomery because that's the one I like."

He turned to consult his idol. "Which one do you like?"

"Both."

"You like Mont*gomery*?"

"I didn't when I was your age. I like it better now."

Tex blew out a breath. "Well, *I'm* calling you Mister Monty, no matter what!"

"Alrighty, then. You have your special name for me and your mother has hers." Amusement flickered in his blue eyes as he gazed at her. "I'm good with that."

So charming. Did he have to be charming on top of everything else? How was she supposed to keep her distance from this man when all she could think of was kissing him? When she was constantly dreaming up ways they could be alone?

She'd considered sticking her lipstick in her pocket. Should have.

11

Monty had hoped for a trouble-free birth and thankfully it had been exactly that. Speckles had passed the placenta with no issues and her foal was nursing like a champ.

The celebratory picnic in the barn featured dried-out meatloaf and cold baked potatoes, but nobody cared. They toasted the addition to "the herd" with beer for Graham and Zinnia, while he and Tex drank ginger ale. Everybody drank from the bottle like real cowboys according to Tex.

Zinnia and Graham cleared away the dishes while he and Tex held down the fort. When they came back, phone numbers were exchanged and they shared pictures and videos. No drama. Just how he liked it.

Then all hell broke loose when Zinnia announced it was Tex's bedtime. He wanted to sleep in the barn and Zinnia wasn't about to let him.

As the little boy dissolved into tears, Graham stayed out of it. Monty took his cue from Graham and ambled away. Except he had a solution, damn it.

Should he interfere? Yeah. He raised his voice so he could be heard over Tex's wails. "Zinnia, can I talk to you for a minute?"

"Can it wait until I put Tex to bed?" She hoisted him off the stool as he sobbed and begged her to let him stay.

"About that. I have a thought if you'd like to hear it."

She gave him a sharp look. Clearly she didn't appreciate his attempt to meddle in her parenting style.

Fair enough. He had no experience with childrearing. But he was a whiz at conflict resolution. He lifted his eyebrows and tilted his head toward the barn's open doors.

Heaving a sigh, she set Tex back on his stool and met him just outside the barn door. "What?"

"He could sleep on my cot."

"How would that help? I can't leave him out here alone. I'm not willing to sleep in the barn and neither is Graham."

"I'm planning to stay all night."

"Why? Everything's going fine." Her breathing quickened. "Is there a problem? Is there something you haven't—"

"No, no. Easy." He instinctively laid his hands on her shoulders to calm her down. But he immediately let go. That contact felt too damn good. "They're both doing great."

The panic in her eyes gave way to wariness. "Then what reason is there for you to stay?"

"The first 24 hours are the most critical for a newborn. And Speckles has never been through this. I don't expect anything to happen, but I want to keep watch to make sure nothing does."

"But if I let him sleep here tonight, he'll want to do it tomorrow night, and the night after that. It sets a bad precedent."

"Does he keep his promises?"

"Mostly. He definitely would if he promised you."

The last part made him uneasy, but he might as well press his advantage and end the crisis. "Then you could tell him I need his help watching his foal tonight and I'll get him to promise me he won't ask to sleep in the barn after tonight. I'll emphasize it's a one-time thing."

She hesitated. "I hate to make you babysit my son."

"It won't be tough duty. He's already sleepy. Or he was until this kerfuffle."

"But if he's on the cot, where will you sleep? I assume you were going to take a few cat naps."

"I have a bedroll in the truck. That's good enough."

"Then give him the bedroll and you take the cot."

"You know I'm not doing that."

"I suppose I do. All right, we'll handle it your way. Just so you know, he usually doesn't defy me like this. He's a good boy."

"I can tell he is. And he's gonna cherish this foal. It's actually a good sign that he wants to stay here tonight. It's more evidence that he and... Monty... will bond quickly."

She snorted. "I thought you weren't going to say his name."

"Decided to try it out."

"And?"

"Still weird. C'mon. Let's go spread the good news."

She turned and started back. "I'll bring out extra blankets."

"That would be nice. Thanks."

"And a couple of pillows."

"Don't go spoiling us. We're two tough cowboys."

"Don't I know it."

Tex sat upright like a little soldier braced for battle, resignation on his tear-streaked face. He'd fallen in love with that foal and he hadn't even been allowed to touch him yet.

Watching that boy and his horse get to know each other would be.... No. He'd best derail that train of thought pronto. He'd help Zinnia through this foaling thing and then make himself scarce.

Tex would get so wrapped up in his Appy that his obsession with him, the first cowboy he'd come to know, would fade. The birthday party would help, too. He might shift his allegiance to Zay, or better yet, Rio, who'd been given the most cowboy name of them all.

Zinnia rested her hands on Tex's narrow shoulders. "I just found out that Montgomery will be staying in the barn tonight and needs an assistant to help him keep an eye on Speckles and her baby. Would you like that job?"

His eyes widened and he nodded vigorously.

She stepped back. "But first you have to agree to the rules."

"What rules?"

Monty took her place and gazed into those solemn green eyes. "Staying with me tonight is a special privilege, sport, a one-time deal. Promise me you won't ask your mother to let you do it again."

"I promise."

"Then let's shake on it." He held out his hand.

Meeting his gaze, Tex put his hand, still damp from wiping away tears, in Monty's much bigger one.

The absolute trust in those green eyes was breathtaking. Was he worthy of it? Big question.

His hand swallowed up Tex's, but together they made the handshake work even better than their first one. "Thanks, Tex. I appreciate your help."

"You're welcome, Mister Monty."

"Let's set up the cot."

"I gots to brush my teeth."

"Oh. Of course you do." He glanced at Zinnia.

"And change into your PJs, sweetie."

"And go potty, Mommy."

"Then we'd better head inside and take care of all that."

"But I'm coming back out, right?"

"You are. I promise." She started to lift him off the stool.

"Wait! I gots to tell Speckles and Monty I'm leaving." Getting to his knees, he peered into the stall. "Don't worry. I'll be rrright back!" He slid quickly off the stool and made for the barn door. "Let's go, Mommy!"

Graham gazed after them as they disappeared into the night. "Nice work."

"I couldn't stand to see him so unhappy."

"Yeah, I figured that was torture for you. You have the softest heart of anyone I know."

"And the softest head. I should be discouraging this hero-worship he's got going on. Instead I'm leaning into it."

"You don't enjoy having a little kid dote on you?"

"Sure! Who wouldn't? But I worry that he'll get too attached."

"Would that be a bad thing?"

"Not on the face of it, but..."

"You're attracted to Zinnia."

"Yessir." He took a breath. "I'm gonna be honest with you, Graham. I'm not ready to jump into fatherhood, especially with a five-year-old."

"I'd say that's a natural reaction."

"I have no experience with kids. I'm sure it's different when you start out with a baby. You learn as you go. But a five-year-old? I wouldn't know what to do."

"Really? Just now you seemed to know exactly what to do."

"Because I'm a middle kid in a large family. We're the peacekeepers. Just because I could figure out this one situation doesn't mean I could do it all the time."

"Just to put your mind at ease, Zin is as leery of this deal as you are. She doesn't want to get involved, either."

"I know. But the chemistry's there, so our best bet is to avoid spending time together. Which means I won't be seeing Tex much, either. That's why I don't want him getting too attached."

"Sounds like you have a plan."

"Um, yeah." Making it up as he went along.

"How come she's calling you Montgomery? Have you already discussed—"

"No. She was searching for a way to handle the foal and me having the same name. She doesn't like calling me Mister Monty like Tex does. I suggested Montgomery."

"You did, huh?"

He shrugged. "Seemed like the obvious answer."

"The name thing won't be much of a problem if you two are intent on avoiding each other."

"Guess you're right." What a depressing thought.

12

After applying more lipstick and shoving the tube in her jeans pocket, Zinnia gathered up a couple of quilts and two pillows. Time to check on Tex.

He was proud of being able to dress and undress himself and she'd left him alone to accomplish that. He should be in his cowboy-themed pjs by now.

He stood in the middle of his room wearing his pjs, boots, jacket and hat. He glanced at her, then returned his attention to his bed.

"Changed your mind, sweetie?"

"Nope. But Smokey wants to go."

"Then he should." Mari had gifted him the iconic plush bear for his second birthday and he'd slept with that cuddly mascot ever since.

"Cowboys don't sleep with bears."

"Are you sure about that?"

He nodded.

"What if you take him and ask Mister Monty about it? If he says they don't, then I'll bring him back inside for you."

"Okay." He grabbed his bear and hugged him tight. "Let's go, Smokey."

Once they were outside, he ran ahead and she swallowed an automatic *be careful.* She'd been raised to take care of herself and she wanted the same for him.

But what she wouldn't give for the chance to ask her parents for advice. Sometimes she consulted Uncle Graham, but he'd never had kids and admitted he wasn't as knowledgeable as her folks would've been.

She gazed up at the stars twinkling overhead. "Miss you guys." She liked to think they could hear her, and that sometimes, when she followed her instincts regarding Tex, they were guiding her.

He got to the barn door first, which was closed to hold in the heat from the sunny day. The night had turned chilly enough to make her shiver. She should have copied her son and put on a jacket. Hadn't thought of it. Too busy deciding how long she should stay at the barn. Not long.

Tex didn't have the strength to slide the door open, so he pounded on it and called out to the men inside. Made her smile. He could have waited for her to open it, but that wasn't his style. He liked having agency over a situation. She encouraged that as much as possible.

She'd never left him with anyone but Mari or Graham. But tonight she was entrusting him to a man she'd met just this morning. She had no hesitation about doing it, though. Monty would watch over her kid with the same dedication he'd afforded Speckles and her foal.

Montgomery. She was having trouble making the name switch. Did it even matter? How often would she need to call him by name? Once this episode was over, she wouldn't be seeing much of him other than at the birthday party.

The muffled conversation and laughter behind the door stopped and Uncle Graham pushed the door open. "Hey, Monty, there's a cowboy out here who's hankering to join us. You okay with that?"

"Always got room for another cowboy," Monty called back.

She quickened her step. "How about a cowgirl?"

"Long as she doesn't mind hanging out with three cowpokes."

"I think I can handle it." She followed Tex inside the cozy interior lit by a couple of electric lanterns. Monty's cot was set up on the far side of the stall door, away from the light.

Monty's gaze fell on Tex's bear. "Looks like this cowpoke brought a friend along."

"It's Smokey. I gots to ask you something."

"Shoot."

"Do cowboys sleep with bears?"

"They sure would if they had one like Smokey. He's a very famous bear."

Standing behind Tex, Zinnia gave Monty a thumbs up.

He responded with a wink, the sexy devil.

"Auntie Mari gived him to me."

"Lucky you."

"Want to hold him?"

"If it's okay with you."

Tex lifted him with both hands offering his most cherished treasure. "Here."

"Thank you." At only nine inches tall, Smokey looked much smaller in Monty's grasp. "Hey, there, Smokey. Thank you for warning us to be careful with campfires and matches."

Tex thrust out his arm, his finger pointed at an unseen audience. "Only *you* can prevent forest fires!"

"Nice!" Monty nodded in approval. "You and Smokey make a great team."

"He's not a cowboy."

"Not technically, but a forest ranger is a lot like a cowboy. They ride horses into the backcountry."

"And he gots a hat."

"Sure does. Hey, sport, I was just in the stall with Speckles and her foal. They're both pretty chill. I thought you and your mom might like to go in for a few minutes."

"Can we touch Monty?"

"Maybe. Uncle Graham rounded up a couple of buckets you can sit on. We'll see if he comes to you. Foals are usually curious so there's a chance he will, but it's better if we let him decide."

"I like that idea." Zinnia glanced at him. "Did he come to you?"

"He might have, but I didn't stay long enough to find out."

"How about you, Uncle Graham? Have you been in?"

"Not yet. Thought you and Tex should be first."

"That's very sweet. I'd love to go in. How about you, son?"

"Yes, *ma'am*!" He hopped in excitement.

"You'll have to be very calm and quiet."

Instantly he went still. "I know." He glanced up at Monty. "Can you keep Smokey for me? Horses gots teeth and I—"

"We don't want him chewed. I'll keep him out here."

"Thank you."

"Glad to. Ready?"

Zinnia put her hand on Tex's shoulder, just in case. "Ready."

"Keep your movements slow and steady." He rolled back the stall door.

"Got it." She knew his instructions were for Tex, who could easily forget himself once he was inside the stall with the foal.

Her mare's ears pricked forward as they walked in. "Hey, girl. Can we come see your baby?"

She nickered softly.

"She said yes, Mommy."

"She did." Behind them, Monty slowly closed the door. She perched on the right-hand bucket. "Sit down as slowly as you can. We don't want to startle either of them."

He eased onto his bucket. "Can we call to Monty?"

"Let's not. Let's just sit here quietly."

"Okay."

"Hold onto your knees. That way you won't be tempted to reach out and touch him if he comes over."

"I hope he comes over."

"I hope so, too, but we have to be patient."

"Here comes Speckles, Mommy."

"Figured she would."

"Can I touch her?"

"Of course, but if she walks away, put your hands back on your knees."

He nodded.

Speckles wandered closer, and after glancing back to where her baby stood, she lowered her head and accepted their nose rubs and chin scratches.

Tex's voice rippled with excitement. "He's watching us."

"He is." That wobbling little creature fascinated her. She'd seen foals before but never one that was only hours old. "What do you suppose he's thinking?"

"He's thinking why are we sitting on buckets."

"Could be."

The foal sneezed, Tex automatically said *bless you* and Speckles left them to check on her baby.

"Does he gots a cold?"

"I doubt it. It's probably that gunk he had over his nose and he has to get it out. He's—"

"*Mommy.*" He grabbed her arm as the foal took a few wobbly steps in their direction.

"Hands on your knees."

Breathing fast, he grabbed his knees so hard his knuckles turned white.

"Deep breaths. If you're too excited, he might not come over."

Inhaling and exhaling through his mouth, he managed to settle himself down, at least a little.

"Good." She gave him a nod of approval.

Then his lips began to move. His soft plea was nearly inaudible. "Come on, Monty. Come on over. Come on over."

He was ignoring her recommendation, but very, very quietly. She decided to let it go.

Maybe that murmur had something to do with the foal's behavior and maybe not. But there was no doubt about it. He was tottering over. Not in a general direction, either.

As if attached to her son by an invisible string, he gradually shortened the distance until he stood squarely in front of Tex.

She held her breath as that beautiful little creature craned his neck, reaching under the cowboy hat to nuzzle her son's ear. Why, oh why hadn't she asked Uncle Graham or Monty to take pictures?

He giggled. The foal stumbled backward, nearly losing his balance. But he righted himself, turned and went to find his mother.

Tex was beside himself. "*Mommy.* He *kissed* my *ear.*"

"He sure did, son. He sure did."

"I didn't mean to laugh, but it tickled. He gots scared. He almost falled down."

"But he didn't. Look, he's fine. He's nursing. He's not upset."

"He wants to be my friend."

"Yes, he does." Victory tasted sweet on her tongue. Her plan was succeeding more spectacularly than she'd dreamed it would. The guilt of choosing the wrong father for her child had already begun to ease.

When she'd decided to breed Speckles, she'd acted on faith that it would work out. She hadn't known she'd end up at Uncle Graham's ranch when the foal was born. But the Universe had been kind to her.

Thanks to her uncle's generosity, she had a home for herself, Tex, her sister, Speckles and this adorable foal. Time, planning and luck had created a solid foundation for raising her beloved son. As long as she stayed the course and didn't go off on a tangent, she had it made.

That meant deep-sixing any fantasies involving Montgomery Bridger.

13

Monty hadn't intended to film the action going on in the stall. But when Tex's lips started moving and the foal responded, he'd pulled out his phone. Zinnia would want pictures.

The video was pure gold and he couldn't wait to show it to her. After the foal returned to his mother, Zinnia and Tex had an excited little confab about the interaction. They both had to be over the moon.

He was on a high, himself. He exchanged a smile with Graham, who'd also taken pictures. This whole deal had to be special for the guy. He'd wanted kids but he'd picked a woman who didn't care for them.

Now he had daily contact with Tex, who was a natural with horses. No doubt Zinnia's influence had enriched that talent. As he helped raise this foal, he'd grow even more intuitive.

What did the future hold for him? Likely he'd be working with horses in some capacity.

Would he become a farrier like his mother and great-uncle? Or a trainer like Jordan? Or a horse whisperer like Luis? Or a vet like him?

That last option created a flare of excitement. Perfectly natural reaction. The profession he loved would benefit. If Tex chose to practice locally, then maybe they could even—

Wait. Wait a damn minute. Somehow his *natural reaction* had ballooned into a future in which he and Tex could be partners. What the hell?

Not long ago he'd promised himself that after this weekend he'd put mental and physical distance between himself and Zinnia's kid. And Zinnia, too.

Especially Zinnia, the curvaceous woman who had finally coaxed her son to leave his seat on the bucket. Rolling back the stall door, she ushered him out. "Any chance one of you guys took pictures?"

Graham held up his phone. "We both did."

"Thank heavens. I didn't think of it until the moment he started over toward Tex."

"And *kissed* me. On my *ear*."

Monty returned his infectious grin. "We saw." He held up his palm and Tex slapped his hand against it. "Congratulations, cowboy."

"Thanks. Now we gots to play cards."

"We do?"

"I didn't bring out the cards. I wasn't sure—"

Graham tucked his phone away. "I'll go get 'em."

"Except Mister Monty doesn't have to play, son. It's polite to ask someone if they want to. Not everybody enjoys card games."

"But he's a cowboy, Mommy. They always play poker."

"You play poker?" He didn't want to insult the kid's intelligence, but that was a complicated—

"It's Go Fish Poker. You gots to match up cards."

"Ah." He swallowed a laugh. "I know that one."

"Hey, I gots an idea!"

"What's that, sport?"

"We can be a team! Me and you against Mommy and Uncle G."

"Sure. As long as it's okay with them." He glanced at Zinnia and his breath hitched. She quickly turned her head, but not before he caught the sheen of tears in her eyes.

"Want to have teams, Mommy?"

She used her sleeve to wipe her eyes and faced them wearing a bright smile. "Teams! What a great idea! You two better bring your A-game because Uncle G and I are in it to win it."

What had brought on those tears? Was he somehow responsible? Whatever had triggered that reaction, she'd conquered it and was fully on board with Go Fish Poker.

Once they started playing, he was the one with concentration issues. He blamed the simplicity of a game that left him plenty of time to gaze at the woman sitting across the card table.

He paid way too much attention to the sound of her breathing, the citrus scent of her perfume, the glisten of the lipstick she'd reapplied. He was distracted by the movement of her nimble fingers and the flush on her cheeks when she scooped up the cards their team won.

Tex saved his butt. The kid had a memory like an elephant, which kept them in a constant tie with their worthy opponents. Zinnia was clearly focused on the game. So was Graham, although Monty caught the guy giving him an assessing look now and then.

Too bad the farrier knew him so well and could spot chinks in his armor. How would this sleepover with Tex work out?

If Zinnia stuck to her guns, she'd skedaddle inside after putting Tex to bed. Or if she didn't, she'd find a reason to keep Graham around.

But Graham was the first to call it a night, maybe because Tex had started to yawn. The teams were tied so Graham agreed to one more game. Monty sharpened his focus for Tex's sake and they broke the tie.

"Good game." Graham stood and stretched. "I'm turning in, but by all means come get me if a problem crops up." He folded up the card table.

"G'night, Uncle G."

"See you in the morning, buddy." Graham leaned down and gave him a hug before picking up the card table and leaving the barn.

"Okay, sleepy boy." Zinnia had fetched Smokey and she held out her hand to Tex. "Smokey's ready to bed down."

"I gots to stay up, Mommy." Tex climbed on his stool. "Me and Mister Monty, we're keeping watch."

Impressive. The kid was yawning and rubbing his eyes, but he'd do his duty. That kind of grit would serve him well in the future.

But in the present, it created a problem. A five-year-old needed sleep.

They needed a reset. "I forgot to explain how this deal works, sport. When you have two cowboys watching over the herd at night, you take turns. I'll handle the first shift. You need to rest up for the second shift."

"Oh." He looked relieved. Climbing back down, he walked over to his mom. "Smokey and me are on second shift. That's how it works."

"I see." She handed him the bear and lifted her head to mouth a silent *thank you.*

He responded with a nod. Then he checked the time on his phone. He'd grab this opportunity to take Speckles' temp and give her a quick exam. The foal's exam could wait until morning.

As he entered the stall, Speckles gave him a glance and went back to munching from her hay net. Evidently he'd earned her trust. She continued eating as he took her temperature and checked for any damage to her tissues from the birth. Nothing major.

Her foal wasn't as trusting and stayed well out of reach. He clearly remembered the man who'd delivered the sting of disinfectant to his navel.

"I know, little one," he murmured. "You'll forgive me eventually. You don't want to hear that it was for your own good, but—" He paused. Was Zinnia singing?

Yes. And Tex was joining in on the chorus of a Kenny Rogers classic, *The Gambler*. He chuckled. Not your usual lullaby, but then Tex wasn't your usual five-year-old.

Good song. Great lyrics. Excellent advice. He'd do well to keep it in mind.

The song ended. Giving Speckles a pat, he left the stall, making as little noise as possible opening and closing the door. At five, his sister Greta had been able to sleep through anything.

He'd never had that ability. Was still a light sleeper. As a baby, or so he'd been told, he wouldn't conk out unless he was in a moving vehicle. Must be true, because he still got drowsy driving at night. Had to blast the radio to stay awake.

He settled down on a hay bale to wait. Would he and Zinnia have that talk? Probably didn't need to. Graham's comments indicated they were already on the same page.

The whisper of her footsteps brought his head up.

"He's out. He's had a long day, so I doubt he'll wake up. You shouldn't have any problems."

"That's good." He got to his feet. "All's well in the stall. Should be a quiet night, then." His crazy heart was thumping so loud he was afraid she could hear it.

"I assume you're not going to wake him up to take his shift."

"Certainly not in the middle of the night." He sounded so calm. Could she tell he was forcing himself to stay planted in this spot, maintaining a safe distance? "But I could wake him up while it's still dark so he can take the last hour before dawn. That way he'll feel like he did his job."

"He'll like that. By the way, thanks for your response to Smokey. I knew you wouldn't make fun of him, but I wasn't sure how you'd handle it without lying."

"I've never taken a poll. For all we know, lots of cowboys take teddy bears to bed with them."

She smiled. "Do you?"

"I used to. I still have Fozzy on a shelf in my bedroom, just in case life gets scary."

"Which house is yours?" Then her cheeks turned pink. "Not that it matters. I was just—"

"I'm in my Grandma Doris's gingerbread cottage. Fozzy fits right in." So would she, if she cared to pay him a visit.

"And she's living in the fuchsia bunkhouse now?"

"Yes, ma'am, along with my three aunties. They call themselves the Dazzling Damsels."

"Uncle Graham told me. I'm glad I'll get to meet them on Saturday."

"You'll have fun. So will Tex."

"For sure." She paused, her expression tough to read. "It was kind of you to include him even though he didn't fit into your original plans."

Ouch. Direct hit. "I..." He gulped in air. "I'm sorry. I took one look at you and I...I have no excuse. I was thinking with my dick."

"You're not the first and you won't be the last."

He groaned. "The thought of being lumped in with every other guy who's lusted after you makes me sick to my stomach."

"You're not lumped in with anybody."

"Of course I am. I deserve to be."

"Not really."

"I've never had that reaction to a woman, and I apologize. Talk about a one-track—"

"Shut the eff up, Montgomery Bridger."

He blinked.

"I can't very well judge you for your behavior when I felt the same way when I first saw you."

He stared at her, speechless. When he finally untangled his vocal cords, his voice was a garbled croak. "I doubt it."

"Oh, no, I promise you I did. But I reined it in. Those thoughts don't fit into my program. You're beautiful, but you're not for me."

She'd called him *beautiful*? "Is that why you were crying a while ago?"

She rolled her eyes. "*No*."

"Something got to you."

"Um, yeah." She glanced away. "The thing is, I picked a loser. It's my fault that Tex doesn't have a dad."

"No, it's not. That guy gets all the blame for—"

"Whether he does or doesn't makes no difference. It's up to me to fix it since he won't. I thought this foal would fill the void. Then I heard the eagerness in Tex's voice when he proposed teaming up with you and I realized...."

His chest tightened. "That foal is a wonderful gift. They'll have a great time together. He's a lucky boy."

She shook her head. "A foal is not enough. He still needs a dad, and I'm not taking a chance on making another mistake." She looked at him, her gaze bleak. "There's no answer."

He ached, and there was nothing sexual about it. Well, maybe slightly sexual. "I wish I could hold you. I wish I could magically make everything better."

"But you could make everything worse. For both of us. For all three of us." She sucked in a breath. "I need to get out of here." Squaring her shoulders, she walked quickly past him.

He resisted the urge to go after her. And do what? She'd said there was no answer. She was probably right.

14

Zinnia couldn't sleep. Big surprise. Who could have predicted that? Ha, ha.

Going to bed when Tex wasn't asleep in his room was unsettling. Wrong. The day would come when he'd ask to spend the night at a friend's house, but this wasn't that day.

He wasn't far away, though. She could easily check on him. Or not so easily. And that was the other reason she lay in the dark, eyes open, wishing Mari would come home so they could talk.

When the front door finally opened and the kitchen light came on, she leaped out of bed and barreled down the hall. "I'm up. I hope you're not exhausted because—"

"Whoa, Zin! Is something wrong?" Mari tossed her backpack on a kitchen chair.

"No, no. Everybody's fine. It's Monty."

"The foal or the cowboy? I saw his truck is still here."

"See? The name's already a problem. I'm calling him Montgomery."

"Which one?"

"The cowboy. I can't change the foal's name. Tex loves it."

"His name's Montgomery? I figured it was Montana."

"No, Montgomery."

"Should I call him that, too?"

"Totally your choice. He said I could use that to avoid confusion, which we're clearly going to have." She studied her sister. "You look tired. I should let you go to bed."

"You look stressed. Let's make cocoa."

"I love you." She hurried to a cupboard. "I'll get the pan."

"I'll get the milk." Mari opened the fridge.

"We haven't done this in a while." The routine soothed her in so many ways. Measuring the ingredients, she heard her mother's voice — *three sugars to one cocoa powder.* The first time she and Mari had made it without supervision, they'd mixed that up and produced something too bitter to drink.

Mari set the milk carton on the counter next to the stove. "We made cocoa Sunday morning."

"That's different." She added water and stirred until she had chocolate syrup. "I meant making it at night before we go to bed, like Mom and Dad used to do."

"Yeah. Not exactly a healthy habit."

"No, but once in a while...."

Mari gave her a sideways hug before taking a couple of mugs from the cabinet above the sink. "Like when you can't sleep."

"For example." She poured in the milk until she had the color they preferred, not too dark, not too pale.

"I should probably go close Tex's door. We don't want him waking up."

"No worries. He's asleep in the barn."

"What?"

"Only because Monty, I mean Montgomery, is out there with him. I emphasized it's a one-time thing."

"Let's hope he gets that. He asked me if his foal can sleep in his room, so be prepared for that request."

"I'll just point out the little deposits that baby leaves in the straw. Should do the trick."

"Is that why you can't sleep? Your baby boy isn't in his bed?"

"That's part of it." She filled the mugs and ran water in the pan while Mari carried the mugs to the sturdy kitchen table Graham had bought thirty-some years ago.

"And Montgomery's the other part."

"Yep." She joined Mari at the table.

"He kissed you."

"Nope. He's been a perfect gentleman."

"You kissed him?"

"I did not."

"But you wanted to."

"So many times. But I can't."

"Because you've forgotten how? I would almost believe that after—"

"Stop it, Mar. You know why I can't. Tex is at a very impressionable age. He already has a crush going on. Monty doesn't want to become a father figure, but if he and I start hanging out together, Tex could start thinking of him that way."

Mari cradled her mug and took a sip, her gaze thoughtful. "So don't hang out together."

"That's my plan, too. I'm going to the party on Saturday, but after that, I won't have much reason to see him. I don't even have to be here when he comes to check on little Monty."

"Little Monty? Is that what you plan to call Speckles' baby?"

"It just came out. Maybe."

"So you'll have Little Monty and Big Monty?"

"Oh, good Lord, no." She laughed. "That's terrible."

"I kinda like it. He is tall, and he probably has a good-sized—"

"Watch it, sis."

"Don't tell me that hasn't been on your mind. Looks to me like Big Monty's the whole package, if you get my meaning."

"I guess we'll never know, since I won't be 'hanging out' with him." She added air quotes.

"You might get the answer if you made a nighttime visit to his house." She took a hefty swallow and put down her mug.

"His *house*? What the hell?"

"Look at it this way." She wrapped her hands around the mug. "You've been celibate for going on four years now. But you don't want to risk another bad marriage and I get that. Big Monty doesn't want to settle down, either, so he's the perfect—"

"Stop calling him that." Her words came out breathy. Mari's outrageous suggestion had gained traction in her fevered brain. But how could it work? She couldn't just—

"If you want to keep it from Uncle Graham and Tex, you'll have to sneak over there on my nights off so I can cover for you if need be. It just so happens I'm off tomorrow night." She glanced at the kitchen clock on the wall. "Or I should say tonight, since it's one o'clock already."

"I couldn't do it, Mar. That's not my style." Meanwhile her deprived libido loudly contradicted that statement.

"Oh, well, then. Forget it. I wouldn't want to interrupt this cloistered life you've chosen just for a delicious romp in the hay with Big Monty." Picking up her mug, she took another drink.

"He strikes me as a straightforward guy. He might not go for something like this."

"Are you kidding me Zinnia Dawn Harrison? Men throw themselves at you! If you show up at his door he'll think he's died and gone to heaven. Oh, but maybe you don't know which door is his. I understand there are multiple dwellings over there."

"I know which one." She gulped. "But I'm not doing it."

"Maybe before he leaves in the morning you should find a moment to run the idea by him and see how he reacts."

"I'm certainly not doing that!"

"Why not?"

"Even if I said something, which I won't, I can see myself chickening out. I don't do this kind of thing, Mar. I just don't."

"Tough times call for tough measures." Mari gestured toward her untouched mug. "Drink up. You're wasting perfectly good cocoa."

She glanced down. No steam. She took a sip. Mostly milk.

"You need a spoon." Mari left the table and crossed to the silverware drawer. "All the chocolate has sunk to the bottom. Which come to think of it, describes your sex life." She returned and handed over a teaspoon. "Come on, scaredy-pants, stir things up."

"It's scaredy-*cat*."

"It can be either. Look it up. And scaredy-pants fits your situation better."

"What if Tex finds out?"

"He won't. It'll only be a couple nights a week. You'll leave after he's asleep and return before he wakes up."

"What if somebody at the Laughing Creek Ranch sees me coming and going?"

"News flash, ranch folks work hard during the day and sleep hard during the night. Leave before dawn and they'll never know you were there."

"Monty wouldn't get a good night's sleep, though."

Mari started laughing. "If you think he gives a damn about that, you haven't been paying attention."

She ducked her head to hide a smile. Her sister was right.

"Are you doing it, then?"

"No. Seriously, it's not me."

15

Monty's plan worked perfectly. He roused Tex before any light showed in the sky and the little guy took his shift. Monty stretched out on his bedroll with his eyes closed, pretending to sleep.

Tex spent the time telling stories to Speckles, her foal, and Smokey, but he kept his voice down. The tales included familiar characters — the Lone Ranger, Hoss Cartright, Bret Maverick, Roy Rogers.

Hard to keep a straight face during that earnest recitation. He'd seen those old shows as a kid, too. They'd probably live forever.

As dawn arrived, shining gently through cracks in the weathered barn walls, he stayed quiet, waiting to see what his young partner would do.

"Sun's comin' up, Smokey." Tex climbed down from his stool, crouched beside the bedroll and patted him on the chest. "Wake up, Mister Monty. It's morning."

He slowly opened his eyes. Tex's face hovered about six inches above his. "It is?"

"Yep! Speckles eated hay and Monty…." He made a sucking noise.

"He was nursing. Perfect. Just what they each should be doing."

"Guess what? You gots a beard! It growed in the night!"

"I'll bet it did."

"Are you gonna shave it? Do you gots that cream? That goes *ppffft* and makes you look like Santa?"

"Not with me, sport."

"Oh, well. You can use Uncle G's."

"Probably better if I wait until I go home. Could you move away a little so I have room to get up?"

"Yep." He settled on his heels, worry clouding his green eyes. "Are you going home now?"

"Not yet."

He sighed in relief. "*That's* good."

Uh-oh. The kid's distress about his inevitable departure was *not* good. Not good at all. Maybe having him stay in the barn all night wasn't such a brilliant plan after all.

Sitting up slowly, he rolled his shoulders to work out the kinks. He hadn't spent the night on a hard surface in years. He'd considered switching to the cot after Tex vacated it, but then he might have dozed off. He wasn't about to do that when Tex was awake.

When he stood, Tex popped up like he was on springs. "We gots to turn out the herd."

"Don't you do that with your Uncle G?"

"But you're a cowboy, too. We can—"

"He's the boss of this outfit. We should wait for him."

"Okay." Clearly not what he had in mind.

"While we wait, I'll check on Speckles and Monty." There, he'd used the foal's name. Progress.

"Can I come in?"

"You sure can after I give them each a quick examination. Just hang out on your stool, please, and I'll be done in a jiffy." If the kid could get involved with his foal, that might ease his separation anxiety.

Fortunately mare and foal were doing great. During the night he'd been able to stealthily clean the stall, at least somewhat, and roll the wheelbarrow out the front door.

Speckles had remained calm through that process, which was a very good sign. He could safely leave them, knowing they didn't need him to monitor their progress. Zinnia, Marigold and Graham could take it from here.

As for Tex, the adorable little boy who'd attached himself like a cocklebur....With luck he'd find such joy in having this foal to love that his neediness would gradually fade.

Just as he was ready to turn the stall over to Tex, the barn door opened. The rest of the family came in, Zinnia in the lead.

Right on schedule, his traitorous body reacted to the visual. What she did for a pair of Wranglers and a blue plaid shirt should be illegal. Adding to the impact, she'd left her hair loose and her curls bounced temptingly against her shoulders. No fair.

"Hey, there." He called a husky greeting and cleared his throat. Maybe she'd think it was the early hour that put that rasp in his voice. "They're in terrific shape." Yeah, that phrase had popped right out. He barreled on. "Tex was just about to go in if anybody would like to join him."

"I'll let Mari go." Zinnia glanced back at her sister. "Since you haven't—"

"Right, and I—oh, my goodness!" She peered into the stall and put a hand to her chest. "If he isn't the most—" She broke off with a little sob and pulled a bandanna from her hip pocket. "Sorry. He's just so…."

"We get it." Zinnia wrapped an arm around her. "We were all bawling last night. Now it's your turn."

"Here's a bucket, Auntie Mari." Tex thrust one in her direction.

Laughter mingled with her tears. "Thanks, but I doubt I'll throw up. I'm just crying happy tears."

"You gots to sit on it."

"I do?"

"You gots to sit and wait for Monty to kiss you."

"Sounds like fun."

Zinnia sighed. "We're talking about the foal, Mar, not the cowboy."

"I knew that." She grinned at him.

He rolled his eyes. *And so it begins.* Time for him to make his escape. "Since everything's going well, I should probably shove off." He tucked everything back in his case and snapped it shut.

His bucket clutched to his chest, Tex swung in his direction. "Are you coming back?"

"Not today, sport."

"Tomorrow?"

He grabbed the best response he could find. "Tomorrow's my birthday."

He brightened. "And the party?"

"Yessir."

"Okay!" His attention shifted to his mother. "Do we gots a present?"

"We'll get one today."

He winced. "Oh, hey, you don't have to get me a—"

"We want to." Zinnia met his gaze. "You've gone above and beyond for Speckles and… Monty." The hesitation was still there, but she used the name.

"I'll add my thanks, too," Graham said. "It meant the world to all of us that you were here."

"It sure did." Mari laid a hand on his arm. "Because you were on duty, I was able to handle my shift without worrying myself sick about things back home. Thank you." She gave his arm a squeeze.

"You're welcome." Something about her smile and the twinkle in her eyes put him on alert. She looked like a woman with a secret. "Glad to do it."

"I'll fold up your cot." Graham walked back to where it sat with a pillow and blankets piled on top.

"I'll get the other stuff." Zinnia followed him.

"C'mon, Auntie Mari." Tex marched over to the stall door. "We gots to go in."

"Be right there." She lowered her voice. "Stay open to the possibilities, my friend."

He frowned. "I don't—"

"You will. I hope." She gave his arm another squeeze before joining Tex and sliding open the stall door.

"Here's the cot." Graham handed it over and clapped him on the shoulder. "Can't even begin to tell you how grateful I am."

"This is the best part of being an equine vet. I love delivering foals."

"Then it's win-win. I'll walk you out to the truck. Oh, and I saw the full wheelbarrow. Thanks for that, too."

"Like I said, above and beyond." Zinnia came toward them holding blankets under one arm and pillows under the other. "I'll walk out with you, too. I have my checkbook in my back pocket."

"Alrighty, then." His mom had advised him to accept the check, which would establish a professional relationship instead of encouraging a personal one. So he'd do that. But he'd give her the family discount.

"Then let me take that bedding off your hands." Graham relieved her of the pillows and blankets. "Where does it go?"

She glanced over her shoulder as she walked out of the barn. "You can leave it on my bed. How're we doing on time?"

"Not bad. We can have breakfast and still make it to the Stevens' place, no problem. I'll start cooking. You're welcome to stay and eat, Monty. I make a mean omelet."

"Appreciate the offer." He stepped out into the warm sunshine. "But I want to get started on that fungus you spotted on Banjo's heel."

"It's not bad yet, but yeah, the sooner the better." He grinned. "Then I'll see you tomorrow, birthday boy."

"About that. Please don't bother getting—"

"Too late. Zinnia and I are on it. Besides, you heard Tex. That kid knows you don't show up to a birthday party empty handed. You wouldn't want to upset him, would you?"

"You got me, there. See you soon." He and Zinnia walked toward his truck and Graham headed up the porch steps.

"I didn't want to ask in front of Tex." Zinnia glanced at him. "Did he sleep okay? Did your plan work?"

"Like a charm." He stowed his case and the folded cot. "He used his early morning shift to entertain the horses and Smokey."

She chuckled. "Stories from old TV shows?"

"Yes, ma'am. Cute as hell."

"I assume you pretended to be asleep."

"Had to. I wanted him to experience being in charge. He did a great job."

"Thank you for that. I held my breath when he asked when you were coming back. He sounded panicked."

"I know. That's exactly what we don't want. Good thing the birthday party distracted him."

"Just so I know, how soon do you have to come back and check on those two?"

"Unless something crops up, not until vaccination time, which is around five months."

"Five months?" She took a breath. "He's gonna drive me nuts asking about you."

"To be honest, I'll miss him, too." And her, but saying that wasn't helpful. He was supposed to work on forgetting this crazy infatuation.

"Five months is a long time at his age."

"Yeah." When he focused on Tex's problem instead of his own, the answer was obvious. "How about this? At lunch yesterday it sounded like Graham misses his visits to the ranch."

"He does seem to love it there."

"Mom picked up on it. I'll bet she'll start specifically inviting him every now and then. She said you were always welcome, so you three could come along."

"That's a good idea. Then Tex won't feel abandoned."

"Abandoned?"

"Think about it. You've become buddies and now you'll disappear for five months. Visits to the ranch will show him you're still buddies. You're just super busy."

"Then I'll mention it to Mom. She'll make sure those visits happen."

"Good. We have a plan."

"Speaking of plans, are you and Mari cooking something up?"

"What do you mean?"

"She said something that made me wonder if there's a secret plan in the works."

She flushed. "Don't pay attention to her. She's always dreaming and scheming." She hesitated. "But now I'm curious. What did she say?"

"*Stay open to the possibilities, my friend.* I started to say I didn't understand when she interrupted me with *You will. I hope.*" He held Zinnia's gaze. "Any clue what she's talking about?"

"Absolutely not." Her flush grew brighter and she broke eye contact.

"Are you sure? Because I think you—"

"I really need to get going or I'll make us late for the Stevens' appointment. How much do I owe you?"

He longed to tell her it was on the house, but he heeded his mom's advice and gave her a figure.

She wrote the check quickly and nicked off the corner when she ripped it out of the checkbook. "Thank you so much. That doesn't sound like enough, but...see you tomorrow!"

"You bet." He folded the check and tucked it in his shirt pocket as she raced away. Something had her flustered. Something to do with him.

He could go back to the barn and try to coax more details from Mari. Except Tex was in there and he'd have to extricate himself a second time.

He'd just have to deal with uncertainty. His least favorite thing.

16

She'd done it to herself. Zinnia wanted to blame Mari for her scrambled thoughts, but the decision to wait up for her sister the night before was all on her. She'd been looking for advice and Mari had given her more than she'd bargained for.

She should have seen it coming. Mari loved to shake things up, and her suggested plan had turned Zinnia's stomach into a cement mixer.

She'd mostly kept her cool while working with Uncle Graham at the Stevens' place. Clearly he'd sensed something wasn't right, though. When he'd asked if she was okay she'd blamed her distraction on lack of sleep. He hadn't pushed it.

They'd finished that job, grabbed lunch at the Raccoon and bought Monty's birthday present at L'Amour and More, the bookshop in the purple Victorian. Another shoeing appointment that afternoon meant they had no time to explore the place, but she'd vowed to get Tex in there soon.

Graham's new clients, a young couple who lived on the outskirts of town, had recently acquired two horses. The shoeing didn't take long, but the couple had very little experience with horses. Over lemonade and cookies, Uncle Graham gave them a shot course in equine care.

She watched as their anxiety faded. After meeting several of her uncle's clients, she had an even greater appreciation for the man who'd stepped in to be both mother and father to her and Mari. Clearly his customers loved him.

The busy day had helped her push aside thoughts of Monty, sometimes for an hour or two. But once they were headed back home, mental images began taunting her.

She replayed the sound of his gentle voice, his laughter, his kind words to her son. Warmth crept through her body as she relived the moment his blue gaze had locked with hers, the message clear.

"Whatdya say we check in with Speckles and Monty?"

Her uncle's question jolted her back to Earth. They were home. "Definitely."

"I've been thinking of Monty off and on all day, wondering how he's doing." He shut off the engine and climbed out.

"Same." She'd balked at the double name issue, but at the moment it covered her response perfectly.

Walking to the barn brought up her last and most potent image of Monty Bridger. Coming through the door this morning, her eyes had taken a moment to adjust from sunlight to shade.

When her vision had cleared, she'd been gifted with a rumpled, bearded, smokin' hot cowboy who'd just climbed out of his bedroll. She'd never get that intimate view again. Unless....

"I'll bet he's steadier than he was this morning."

Oh, he'd looked plenty steady this morning. Steady enough to sweep her up in his strong arms and—oh wait. Her uncle was talking about the foal. "He probably will."

"I can't wait until he's old enough to go out in the pasture. Those videos we found of foals running beside their moms were so doggone cute."

"Yeah, they were."

He pulled out his phone. "I didn't take any this morning, so I'd better do it now. Raquel asked for a few more."

"When was that?"

"Last night, after I sent her some from the birth."

"So you emailed her last night?"

"Email's too slow. I, um, texted them."

She whirled to face him. "You faker! You know how to text!"

He looked like a little kid caught with his hand in the cookie jar. "Doesn't mean I like it. Seemed like I had no choice."

"I'll bet you surprised the heck out of her."

He chuckled. "Yeah."

Ding, ding, ding. It was official. Her uncle had a crush on Raquel, a significant one if he'd taught himself to text. She wanted to tease him but held back.

He might not have admitted it to himself yet. Better to leave it alone. He likely didn't want to discuss his situation any more than she wanted to discuss hers.

"Well, it was very thoughtful of you to text her instead of calling. Let's go get those videos so she won't have to wait any longer."

"Monty probably showed her some already." He fell into step beside her.

"But those would be old. You can send her something more recent."

"That's my thought."

A crush, for sure. She hurried into the barn ahead of him so he wouldn't see her smile. "Mari? Tex? You guys in here?"

No response other than a short whinny from Speckles.

"I guess they're up at the house."

She leaned on the stall door and Speckles came over, her gaze expectant.

"Hey, girl, I should've stopped by the house and brought carrots." She reached out and scratched under her mane. "I'll just take a peek at your son and then go get some."

"He looks good." Uncle Graham propped his arms on the stall door and gazed at Monty, who'd followed his mom over but stood a couple of feet back, his stubby tail switching back and forth

"He does look good. Love those markings."

"Like someone flung paint on his haunches."

"I wanted to name him Rorschach, but I knew Tex would never go for it."

"That's for sure."

"When did Monty take off Speckles' tail wrap? Was it gone this morning?"

"I think so. He probably took it off last night."

She'd been so focused on that cowboy she hadn't noticed. She also hadn't absorbed the reality of this foal.

Now that he was here, she had questions. She'd read up on training a foal, but she'd also be in charge of teaching her son the basics. She wanted him involved in those training sessions. Too bad she'd decided to minimize contact with Monty, who'd be a great source of information.

"Want to go in?"

"I don't need to. It's nice just watching them."

"Mari must've done a little more cleaning. Doesn't look too bad, considering."

"In the morning we could move them to a different stall and do a thorough job."

"Good idea." He gave her a sideways glance. "Whatcha thinking, Zin?"

"This little colt is a blank slate and I've never trained a foal before. Plus I need to include Tex in the program, and I'm not sure how to do that, either."

"You gonna monopolize that job?"

She looked over and caught his smile. "No, of course not."

"I admit I've never trained a foal or trained a kid in how to do it. Neither has Mari, but we're all reasonably intelligent. I wager we'll figure it out."

"We will." But it sure would be nice to talk to Monty every now and then. If they stuck with the program they'd decided on, family visits to Laughing Creek every so often, that wouldn't give her enough access on a regular basis.

But if she had the courage to take Mari's advice, she'd have all kinds of access. She wouldn't be doing it just for herself. She'd gather information that would benefit Tex.

Oh, who was she kidding? She didn't have to become Monty's lover to tap him for that knowledge. She could text him questions and he'd text answers. Neat. Clean. Impersonal.

If she chose to drive over to Laughing Creek tonight, she'd be doing it because she didn't want to lose the chance to make love to the only man she'd wanted from the minute she'd laid eyes on him.

17

Monty flipped back the covers, turned off the bedside lamp and stretched out naked in the middle of his king-sized bed. Flinging his arms wide, he stared up at the rafters faintly visible above him.

His skin was still damp from his second shower of the day. A soft breeze through the open window made him shiver, but he didn't pull up the sheet. The night was warm. He welcomed the cool caress.

He'd showered and shaved after arriving home this morning. Then he'd worked like a maniac all day to make sure nothing critical would be left hanging during his birthday celebration.

Bridgers did not labor on the anniversary of their birth. It was family law, a law he'd come to appreciate since he'd turned into something of a workaholic.

But he'd pushed himself harder than usual today. Staying busy helped take his mind off Zinnia. No distractions now, though, other than the chirp of crickets in the wild rose bush outside his window.

It had grown above the sill and needed trimming, but that meant cutting off some of the fragrant flowers. Did Zinnia like bouquets? He'd never know.

He sighed and closed his eyes. And there she was in exquisite detail—vivid green eyes, full pink lips, wavy golden hair, luxurious breasts, narrow waist, tempting ass, slender legs.

He didn't need to see her naked to imagine how she'd look. His cock responded, and for a split second he considered doing something about that condition. But he knew from experience the satisfaction would be short-lived and hollow.

Twenty-four hours ago he'd struggled to fall asleep lying on a wooden barn floor with only a folded blanket under him. His thick, cushy mattress was a hundred times more comfortable, but he'd rather be back on the barn floor, anticipating Zinnia's arrival in the morning.

That type of interaction was over. He'd see her tomorrow at the party, but only in snatches and never alone. He was the star of the show, which meant no sneaking off into dark corners for a cozy chat. No gazing into those emerald eyes and fighting the urge to kiss her.

At the time he'd cursed the frustration of those moments. Turned out he'd take frustration over absence any day. The occasional visits they'd talked about might be enough for Tex, but not for him. He was gonna miss her like the devil.

That depressing thought took care of his woody. With a big day tomorrow, he needed sleep after lying awake most of last night. Folks called him heroic for pulling those all-nighters while tending to a patient. No problem for a card-carrying insomniac.

Only two remedies worked consistently and he didn't have access to either one. He'd been trying out a third one and the results were mixed. Still, it was worth a shot.

Starting at the top of his head, he tensed and released muscle groups all the way down to his toes. He imagined himself sinking into the mattress, surrendering control. Gradually the chirp of the crickets and the scent of roses faded.

Tap. Tap. Tap.

Awareness returned. He kept his eyes closed. Probably wind blowing a tree branch against the porch.

Tap. Tap. Tap.

Damn wind.

Tap-tap-tap-tap-tap-tap.

What the hell? A branch wouldn't do that unless the wind was howling, which it wasn't. He sat up.

A woodpecker? They didn't work at night, did they? The only people who'd summon him at this hour were family members and they'd knock. This rapid tapping thing was the work of a critter.

Oh, well. Wasn't happening, now. Maybe he'd attracted an insomniac woodpecker but now they'd flown away. Flopping down, he closed his eyes.

He'd have to do the blasted tense-and-release routine all over again. He squeezed and released his eye muscles, clenched and released his jaw, hunched and dropped his shoulders—

Tap-tap-tap.

"Damn it!" Vaulting out of bed, he stormed into the living room. "Whatever's doing that better hightail it out of here before I—"

"It's me."

A person? He covered his crotch and took a step back. "Who's me?"

"Zinnia."

"*Zinnia*?" His brain turned into a pinball machine. "Is something wrong with Speckles? Or Monty?"

"Shhh! They're fine. Let me in. Quick."

"Just a sec." He hotfooted it back to his bedroom and struggled into a pair of sweats. She could have opened the door herself and come in. It wasn't locked. Why hadn't he said that?

Because he needed pants first. Why was she out there if her horses were fine? Surely she wasn't.... But what if she was? What if she—

"Hurry."

"I am. I just—" He couldn't seem to tie the drawstring so he just left it. The waistband sagged around his hips as he padded to the door and opened it.

She barreled past him wearing flip-flops judging from the slap of rubber on the wood floor. "Close the door. Quietly."

He eased it shut, leaving them mostly in the dark. The glow from the porch light seeped into the room, giving him a shadowy view. Her flimsy tank top and shorts looked like nightwear. A purse with a long thin strap hung from her shoulder.

Was she about to proposition him? His cock surged to life.

"I woke you up." Her voice was a little shaky. "I'm sorry."

"You didn't wake me up. Why are you here?"

Her breath hitched. "Isn't it obvious?"

"Not really. Seductions don't generally begin with an apology."

"How are they supposed to start? I've never been the one to make the first move."

He stared at her as all his blood traveled south. "Are you serious?"

"Yes. I want..." She gulped. "I mean, I would really like..." Shaking her head, she muttered a curse. "Would you please have sex with me?"

His body answered immediately but his brain was still trying to catch up. "What about Tex? I thought you—"

"He never has to know."

"*Somebody* has to know. You can't just sneak over here without telling—"

"Mari knows. It was her idea."

He was getting the picture. That's why she'd told him to stay open to the possibilities. "What if Tex wakes up and goes looking for you?"

"He's a champion sleeper." Her words came out in a nervous rush. "But if he wakes up and finds me gone, he'll go to Mari. She'll say—" She put a hand to her chest and sucked in air. "She'll say I'm checking on Monty and I'll be back soon."

His eyes had adjusted to the dim light. She was braless and likely panty-less under her outfit. Message received. This was a booty call, and he was going to answer it.

Her cover story for Tex was a riot. "Checking on Monty, are you?"

"It's not exactly a lie. How was your day?"

He choked out a laugh. "Kind of boring until a gorgeous woman showed up at my door asking for sex."

"She sounds a little pushy."

"Fine with me. I like assertive women. By the way, is it a one-night stand? I'd like to know in advance."

"That depends."

"Is this an audition? That's not a game-changer, but—"

"No! I'd *never* ask for a sexual trial run!" She clapped her hand over her mouth and glanced at the open porch window. "I hope nobody heard that."

He smiled. "Besides me?"

"You know who I mean. Does everyone keep their windows open?"

"Probably, but they're all sawing logs by now. I'm the only one in the family who has a problem sleeping."

"Insomnia?"

"Yep. Ever since I was born, I'm told."

"Me, too."

"Is *that* why you're here? Sex helps you sleep?" Would he let her use him in place of a pill? Yes, he would.

"You think I'd take this crazy risk simply to get a decent night's sleep?"

"I guess not. But I gathered you'd closed up shop to focus on Tex. So why me? Why now?" He shouldn't care. He should quit asking questions and take her to bed. If it was for one night only, so be it.

"I've never had such a strong reaction to a man and you've said this is a first for you. It seems a shame not to at least...." She took a quick breath. "At least find out."

He absorbed the significance of her shift in thinking. After several years of celibacy, she was making an exception. He figured she'd wrestled with the idea before driving over here. "Do you have a plan?"

"A potential plan." She swallowed. "Mari offered to cover for me on her nights off."

"Then it's *not* a one-night stand." His heart swelled with anticipation and... joy. She wanted to be with him, even if that meant breaking her self-imposed rule and keeping a secret from her son and her uncle.

"That's up to you. if you'd rather make this short and sweet, just to stay on the safe side, then I—"

"No, ma'am." There was no safe side when it came to this woman. "I'll take whatever you're willing to give for as long as you're willing to give it."

18

In the dim light Zinnia couldn't see the gleam in Monty's eyes, but his tone was the same one he'd used when he'd taken on Speckles' foaling. He was all in.

Thrilling. Scary, too, because now the conversation was over. It was go-time. Her fingers trembled as she unzipped her small cross-body bag. "I thought you might not be prepared, so I brought—"

"Very thoughtful. Let me take that."

She handed him the bag. "Then I was right?"

"You would've been a week ago." He set her bag on the nearest chair. "You were smart to bring some."

"You picked up condoms a week ago?"

"Yes, but—"

"Listen, if there's someone you—"

"I'm not dating anyone right now. It was a random purchase. I might have had a premonition."

"About me? Did Uncle Graham say something that made you think we'd get along?"

"He only told Mom he'd taken you on as his assistant. Didn't mention any details. I wasn't the least bit prepared for the woman who stepped out of his truck." He held out his hand. "But I am now. Come with me, pretty lady."

She inhaled and slowly let the air seep from her lungs. This was it. Once she took his hand, there was no turning back.

She slid her fingers through his, absorbed the warmth and strength in his hand, and immediately started shaking. What was she doing? What if Tex had a bad dream and wanted Mari to go bring her back from the barn? What if Uncle Graham got up for a drink of water and saw her truck was gone?

Tightening his grip, Monty pulled her close. "On second thought, I don't want to wait another minute for this."

Contact with his deliciously bare chest increased her panic. She could still back out, say she'd made a mistake. She'd be home before Tex or Uncle Graham missed her.

"Thinking of making a run for it?"

The rapid pulse of his heartbeat against her chest reminded her she was playing with fire. "I know I started this, but...."

"Now you're getting cold feet?"

She tipped her face up to his. "Yeah. I feel like a fool for saying that. I made the decision and now—"

"Want to go home?" He loosened his grip on her hand.

She sucked in a breath. Relief battled regret. "I really should."

"Can I kiss you goodbye before you leave?"

She'd been wanting to kiss him ever since yesterday morning. One kiss, then she'd leave. "Um, okay."

"Thank you." Leaning down, he brushed his lips over hers, his warm breath carrying a whiff of mint.

She tensed. That was only the preamble. The real kiss would be quite different.

He lifted his head. "I've wanted to kiss you ever since yesterday morning."

"I've wanted to kiss you, too." The scent of soap and lusty male was a powerful aphrodisiac, but she'd have a much calmer life if she abandoned this wild scheme while she still could. As soon as he finished kissing her, she'd be outta here.

Except he seemed in no rush to continue. "Was that it, then? The goodbye kiss?"

He looked surprised. "You didn't like it?"

"It wasn't quite what I expected."

"Sorry about that. Let me try again." His mouth settled on hers.

He was still taking it easy. Gently those velvet lips coaxed her to open to him. That was fair. After all, this would be their one and only kiss.

If he wanted to get tongues involved, that was reasonable. They'd never do this again and it felt so good. She couldn't help kissing him back, couldn't stop herself from slackening her jaw and inviting him to go deeper.

With a soft groan, he accepted that invitation, pulling her closer, sliding both hands to her backside and bringing her in tight against his very hard cock.

A persistent throb of desire began in her core and spread like lava, heating her body, relaxing her tense muscles and taunting her with what she'd give up when she walked out that door.

He lifted his mouth a fraction, his breath coming fast, his voice gruff with passion. "Don't go. Let me love you."

His urgent plea landed like a rocket in her midsection, bringing a rush of moisture and an ache that he'd be happy to address if she said the word. She wanted... oh, how she wanted... but Tex....

But *this.* She'd spend the rest of her life wondering what being loved by Monty Bridger would have been like. Tex would grow up, find his own special person, and she'd have... so many regrets.

She sucked in air and let it out slowly. "I'm staying."

"Thank God." Tightening his grip on her tush, he picked her up. "Wrap your legs around me."

"Hey, I'm heavy. I can—"

"I gots you."

That startled a laugh out of her and wiped away the last of her misgivings. She wrapped her legs around his hips as he headed down the hall.

How effortlessly he cradled her against his lightly furred chest. The song *Holding Out for a Hero* played in her lust-scorched brain.

His dark, erotically scented bedroom teased her with the delicacy of wild rose, the tang of Ivory soap and the musky aroma of sex. The vague outline of a ginormous bed and rumpled sheets ramped up the drumbeat of arousal. She'd never been so turned on in her life.

Lowering her to the smooth expanse, he followed her down, his big body covering hers, his fleece-covered groin wedged between her trembling thighs. He balanced his weight on his forearms. "You drive me crazy."

"Works both ways." She unhooked her arms from around his neck and hugged his muscled torso. "I love the way you feel. You're so *solid*."

"Especially here." He rocked forward, his cock pressed firmly against the damp material of her pj bottoms.

An enthusiastic response from her core sent a warning. "Um, you might wanna get out of your—"

"Yes, ma'am. But first, how about some light?"

"Sure."

"Close your eyes."

She squeezed them shut as he shifted his weight and clicked a switch.

"Wow."

Slowly opening her eyes, she gazed into his. So blue. So filled with awe.

He dragged in a breath. "I can't believe you're here. That you're in my bed. That your hair's spread out on my pillow."

"I can't believe it, either. I can't believe I can finally touch you."

"Please do." His voice was thick, his breathing uneven.

When she began stroking the bunched muscles of his back, he shivered. "Are you ticklish?"

"No, I just..." His chest heaved. "I've never been so...."

"Me, either." Moving her caress lower, she slipped both hands under the loose waistband of his sweats, cupped his ass and squeezed. Oh, baby.

He gasped. "Careful." He backed away. "Time to ditch these." Leaving the bed, he shoved down his sweats and kicked them away.

She sat up and watched. Oh, did she ever. She hadn't seen a naked man in ages, and she'd never seen one equipped like Monty Bridger.

He took a step toward the bed. "Let me take off your—"

"Never mind me. Just locate those condoms you bought last week."

"Yes, ma'am."

She pulled her tank top over her head only to find he hadn't moved an inch. He stood frozen in place, his entire focus on her chest.

Ah. She'd forgotten she could immobilize a man with a scooped-neck shirt and lobotomize him if she took it off.

He blinked, shook his head and gave her a sheepish glance. "Sorry. You're probably sick to death of guys reacting like that."

He got it? That was new. "Yeah, but you're the first one who's apologized. Besides, I ogled you just now. You're probably sick of that, too."

He smiled. "No." Holding her gaze, he came over and sat on the bed. "You were disappointed when I stared. I saw it in your face."

"Which means you switched gears and looked at my face. That puts you in a different category right there."

"And I'm looking at your face now." He slipped his hand under her hair and cupped the back of her neck. "You have world-class breasts, but I want to make love to all of you. Maybe you don't even like to be touched there."

"Well..." He was quickly rising above the level of every male she'd ever allowed to kiss her, let alone the few who had been permitted more than that. "I do like it, but not if a man is...."

"Obsessed?"

"Yes. Exactly."

"I promise not to be that man."

Her heart cherished his promise, cherished it hard. She could fall for this cowboy. She hadn't factored that in. She'd be wise to do so.

19

If Monty had been given time to think about it, he likely would have figured out that zeroing in on Zinnia's considerable assets was a mistake. That said, her unexpected arrival tonight had turned his brain to limp noodles and taken his cock in the opposite direction. It was a wonder he was making any sense at all.

Yes, he'd been stunned by the sight of her generous, perfectly formed breasts tipped with rosy nipples. And his reaction had marked him as just another unevolved male with a boob fetish.

But judging by the sparkle in her green eyes when she'd urged him to suit up ASAP, not to mention the speed with which she'd wiggled out of her pants, he'd redeemed himself.

He rolled the condom into place and glanced at her. Taking a moment to capture the image, he resisted the urge to pinch himself. So beautiful. She lay on her side, her head propped on her hand, likely so she could watch him complete that operation.

She quickly lifted her gaze. "I just wanted to make sure you put it on right."

That made him chuckle. "My cock has already lost its fascination for you?"

"Uh, not exactly." She flushed. "But fair is fair. I don't want to be a hypocrite."

"What if I like being ogled?" He slid onto the bed and mirrored her position. "What if it turns me on?"

"Does it?"

"Uh-huh." Threading his fingers through her hair, he relished the springy texture as he combed it behind her ear. "Your eyes go from emerald green to forest green. That's sexy."

Her breath hitched. "Everything about you is sexy."

"Glad you think so." Leaning in, he kissed her, keeping it light. Clearly she'd been mauled by clumsy lovers in the past. He didn't really blame them for losing their cool when presented with her magnificent body.

But he wouldn't lose his cool. Leaving her tasty mouth, he feathered kisses along her jawline and nuzzled behind her ear. He had a plan.

"Mmm. Let's get closer." Putting her arm around his waist, she snuggled in, rolled to her back and brought him with her. "That's better."

"Sure is." Oh, right. He was in bed with a woman who had muscles and knew how to use them. She'd caught him off-guard, and now they were skin-to-skin.

He'd automatically braced himself on his forearms so he wouldn't crush the breath out of her, but she had him in a tight hold. No daylight between his chest and her spectacular breasts. Plump. Warm. Silky.

A wave of primitive hunger hit with a vengeance. Moisture pooled in his mouth. His fingers curled. He wanted to feel the weight in his palm, feast on all that bounty, bury his face in—no, damn it!

"Your eyes go dark, too."

"I'm not surprised." He sucked in air. "You're potent." Fighting for sanity, he pushed upward, just enough so he could lean over and kiss her. *Don't look down, boy. Don't look down.* He captured her mouth, going for the gusto this time as he settled his hips between her thighs.

As an alternative, it wasn't half-bad. He loved kissing her. Resting his package inches away from nirvana set off mini-fireworks of anticipation in his highly sensitized body.

Could he proceed without cracking? Maybe he should just ditch the plan and go after what his cock was begging for. He didn't think she'd object.

No, damn it. He'd stick with the plan. He had something to prove to himself. And her.

But she seemed hell-bent on sabotaging his noble effort. She slid her hands south, likely aiming for his ass. If she repeated her previous move, he'd be toast.

Reaching back, he caught one wrist and brought it over her head, holding it there.

That drew a muffled protest.

Breaking the kiss, he murmured in her ear. "If you grab my ass, I'm liable to come."

"Really?"

"Yes, ma'am."

"If you're that close, we should—"

"We will." Releasing her wrist, he lifted his head and gazed into her eyes. "There's something I want to do first."

She frowned. "Something kinky? Because I'm not into that."

"Not kinky. Nice."

"Am I supposed to do anything?"

"Just close your eyes."

"All right." Her lashes fluttered down.

Now he was free to look. He hadn't intended that, but.... Heart pounding, he surveyed the territory.

Clearly sunlight had never fallen on those glorious breasts. A faint tan line marked the boundary of a swimsuit. He counted three small freckles, one above her left nipple and two on the underside of her right breast.

"You're so beautiful."

Her breath hitched and her pink nipples tightened, changing to dark rose.

"So beautiful." Closing his eyes, he placed a kiss in the hollow of her throat. Then he created a line of kisses between her breasts.

Their fullness brushed his cheeks. *Stay focused, dude.* She lay very still, her breathing quick and shallow. Was she waiting for him to lose control?

Scooting down, he cradled both breasts in his cupped hands and kissed a wide circle around each nipple. Then he used the tip of his tongue to moisten those tempting buds.

The sound of blood rushing in his ears almost made him miss her faint whimper. "Zinnia?"

"Don't stop." Her voice was breathy. "This is lovely."

Encouraged, he drew a nipple gently into his mouth.

"More."

He began to suck, taking it easy, banking his hunger.

"*More.*"

Okay, then. He loosened the reins just a little and concentrated on giving her pleasure, not wallowing in his.

She arched into his caress and urged him on, clearly enjoying the heck out of his approach. Hallelujah.

His groin ached like crazy, but he'd keep this up until she called a halt. Which she did, reaching for him and making a clear, earthy request.

He gladly complied, burying his cock in her juicy channel. He almost came. Locking down that response, he paused, anchoring his attention on her luminous eyes and flushed cheeks. "I need a second."

She gulped for air. "You can have at least two."

"Just need the one." Holding her gaze, he began to stroke. "We can't be loud."

"I know." Breathing fast, her hands on his hips, she rose to meet him. The glow in her eyes intensified each time he drove home.

Home. He'd met her yesterday. They should be awkward with each other. They weren't. Not even a little.

When he looked into her eyes, she looked right back. No barriers.

They trusted each other. Simple as that. He would come soon and so would she. They would share the most intimate experience two people could have, and he wanted it. Wanted it more than he ever had before.

Her body tensed. Her eyes widened. Now. When her first spasm hit, he hurled himself over the edge. Gasping and shaking, bathed in glory, they shared the freefall and gently touched down.

His world had just shifted. Permanently.

20

"Epic." Zinnia stared up at the first lover who'd made her feel cherished. Monty was one of a kind.

"Sure was."

His soft smile turned her to mush. "Thank you for being so... tender."

"It was my pleasure."

"And mine. For once I didn't feel like a chew toy."

His eyebrows arched. "A chew toy? Yikes. It's a wonder you let me near you."

"I think somehow I knew you would be different. Oh, and next time..." She sucked in air. "Let's close the windows."

He choked on a laugh. "You think?"

"I wanted to yell so bad."

"Me, too."

"I don't care how soundly everyone sleeps, they'd hear that."

"Yeah." He chuckled. "Loud conversation is one thing, but once we were into it, I realized—"

"Nobody sleeps *that* soundly."

"And those sounds are... distinctive." He grinned. "I'll close them right now. I need to get up anyway." And just like that, he was out of bed and headed for the bathroom.

Listening to the splash of water in the sink, she pictured him washing up. She considered following him in there and offering to help. That would be fun. She had yet to get her hands on his impressive bad boy.

Instead she stretched out with a deep sigh of satisfaction, luxuriating in an unfamiliar post-orgasm glow. Turned out a considerate lover made quite a difference. She was relaxed and yet energized.

Maybe she would go in there, after all. But as she sat up, Monty came out of the bathroom. Her breath caught. What a fool she would have been to walk out on this man.

He met her gaze. "I'm going to apologize in advance for the times I slip up and ogle you. I'll do my best, but I'm—"

"Forget about it. You just earned yourself the right to ogle all you want. I intend to do the same."

He chuckled. "You've got a deal." With a complete lack of self-consciousness, he crossed to the window and closed it.

She didn't miss a thing, not the flex of his deltoids or the tightening of his glutes. Poetry in motion.

He turned to face her. "I need to shut the rest of these. Want anything from the kitchen while I'm making the rounds?"

"Water would be great." If someone had asked her to name her favorite side, she might have to choose the frontal view for obvious reasons, but both had their good points.

"Just water? My little sis decided I needed fattening up and brought me a box of sticky buns from her bakery."

"Uncle Graham told me about Greta's coffee shop. I'd hoped to stop in today when we went to—um, to the Raccoon for lunch but we ran out of time." She caught herself before mentioning the bookshop visit. She wanted his gift to be a complete surprise.

"Then water and sticky buns it is." He left the bedroom.

Watching him walk around naked had a predictable effect. She'd just been marveling at her level of relaxed satisfaction. A few minutes spent focused on his muscular body in motion and she was ready to rumble, the sooner the better.

But he was bringing them a snack. And she wanted his advice on next steps with the foal and Tex. Now might be a good time to talk about it.

She'd been vaguely aware of pillows during their recent adventure but hadn't paid them much attention. He'd chosen four regular sized instead of two super-sized ones.

Propping them two-and-two against the curved wooden headboard, she leaned back facing the curved footboard at the end. Interesting that he'd decided on a sleigh bed. Or his grandmother had.

Crowded bookshelves in a matching dark wood sat on either side of the window. Sure enough, he'd made room for Fozzy Bear on the second shelf from the top. A rolltop desk of the same wood, a straight-backed desk chair and an upholstered easy chair in a dark green fabric took up the space on the other side of the room.

Neat, except for his sweats and her pjs lying on the floor. After seeing his efficiently packed medical case, this orderly bedroom didn't surprise her.

Four framed pictures on the top shelf of the desk looked like they might be family photographs. Three were group shots. In the fourth, a woman in boots, jeans and a long-sleeved shirt leaned against a rail fence. She had light hair.

"Sticky buns time." Monty walked in carrying a tray loaded with two tall water glasses and a plate piled high with pastry.

She laughed. "Are you trying to fatten *me* up?"

"No, ma'am. I'm trying to make you glad you knocked on my door."

"I'm already glad. No need to bribe me with pastry."

"Good to hear. Want me to take them back to the kitchen?"

"Not now. I can see them and I can smell them. I crave me some buns." She wiggled her eyebrows.

"Don't I know it." He grinned, gave her the tray and climbed in beside her. "After I walked away and left you alone, I started worrying those second thoughts might come creeping back."

"They didn't." Setting down the tray, she picked up a glass, a napkin and a sticky bun. "I've been absorbing my surroundings. Found your bear. He looks happy."

"He likes it here."

"I can see why. It's a nice room."

"I like it, too. This cottage always appealed to me." He took a sip of water before grabbing a napkin and a sticky bun. "I'm lucky to have it."

"Is the furniture yours or hers?" She bit into her treat. Amazing.

"The bed's mine. The rest used to be hers, but she's given it to me. I've loved that rolltop ever since I was a kid. She loves it, too, but there's no room in the bunkhouse."

"I assume those are pictures of your family?"

"Mm-hm." He nodded, his mouth full of sticky bun.

"Who's the lady on the end?"

He chewed and swallowed. "My mother."

"It is? But—"

"She died in childbirth. Having me."

"Oh." She scrambled for the right thing to say. "That's... is it... I mean, do you feel...."

"Sad? Sometimes. She was so young, the same age I am now."

"That is young. Was your grandma around then?"

"Yes, and I'm sure she was a huge comfort and help to my dad. Then he married Raquel when I was fourteen months old. She's the only mother I've ever known."

"I did wonder why you didn't look like her, but genetics can be wonky."

"Not in your case. Tex looks exactly like you."

"For which I'm grateful. He won't remind me of his worthless father. But the poor kid will have to deal with this hair." She held out a strand of it.

"You don't like it?"

"It's impossible. If I cut it short I look like a blonde Little Orphan Annie. If I let it grow out it looks like I stuck my finger in a light socket."

"And if you let me run my fingers through it, I'll want you all over again."

"What?" She glanced at him. "You like the way it feels?"

"Love it. It's like putting my fingers in a rippling brook."

"Huh." She took another sip of water and finished off her sticky bun. "I can't agree with that, but it's nice of you to say. I'll remember it the next time I'm cussing it out. Thanks."

"You're welcome. Who'd you inherit it from?"

"My dad." She smiled. "He didn't like it, either, so he kept his super short. Then he started going bald. Most men don't like going bald, but he was happy about it."

He gazed at her, his expression touchingly wistful. "I like the way you talk about him. You look... happy."

"It took a while." And he hadn't made it to that place, poor guy.

"I still struggle sometimes."

"Sure you do. You've only had a couple of years. I've had ten. It gets easier."

His chest heaved. "That's what I tell myself. That's what we all tell ourselves."

Reaching over, she squeezed his arm. "You'll get there. He'd want you to be happy, just like my folks would want that for Mari and me."

"Yeah, I know. Listen, speaking about your dad, Graham thought I should share my experience with this name thing." He polished off his sticky bun and picked up another one.

"Which name thing? We have more than one name thing." She grabbed a second pastry, too.

"The Sebastian one. The thing is, when I ditched Montgomery, my dad continued calling me that. Ticked me off when I was younger, but I finally let it go."

"You think I should start calling Tex Sebastian?"

"Not at all. But maybe in a couple of years you might try explaining why you love that name and what it would mean to you if he used it. It could change his perspective. It would've changed mine."

She studied his profile. The hint of tension in his jawline told her this wasn't a comfy subject. "I take it your dad never explained why he hung onto Montgomery."

"Not fully. He just said it was a good name and he wanted to keep using it. I thought he was just being stubborn. He could be stubborn."

"But there was more to it?"

"Yeah. I didn't find out until yesterday when Graham told me."

"Good grief! When did he do that? We had so much going on—"

"When we went to fetch the hay bales before dinner. Seems my mother adored the name Montgomery and swore she'd never shorten it even if others did. My dad kept using the whole thing to honor her memory."

"Why didn't he tell you?"

"I guess because he would have had to talk about her and he avoided doing that. He never really got over her death."

"That's too bad. For him and for you kids."

"It wasn't great. We learned to avoid the subject. My information about her came from my grandma, Adam and Claudie, plus whatever my mom — Raquel — had learned. My grandma says he blames himself, like it was his fault she died."

"Was there any reason why he would?"

"Grandma says absolutely not. Maybe calling an ambulance would have made a difference instead of Dad driving her to the hospital, but she didn't want one and insisted she was fine."

"I can see refusing that option when you're in labor. Who wants sirens and flashing lights?"

"She obviously didn't. She would have had access to medical intervention earlier, but the choice was hers. Nobody predicted it would go bad so fast."

"It sounds like your dad did blame himself, though, if he wasn't able to talk about her."

"Sadly, it makes sense. He was the guy who could do it all — town mayor, home builder, rancher, rescuer of wild horses. But he couldn't save the woman he loved."

"I'm guessing he wasn't the type who'd go see a therapist."

"He'd rather die. Which he did." His chest heaved. "And why the hell did I have to bring this up now? It could have waited. Sorry."

Zinnia picked up the tray and moved it to the bedside table. Then she crawled into his lap, took away his glass and put it on the other nightstand. "You picked the perfect time, Montgomery Bridger. I gots you." Cradling his face in her hands, she kissed him.

21

This woman. Monty groaned as Zinnia's sweet kiss of sympathy gradually turned into an X-rated one that sent an urgent message to his groin. He loved the way she was sucking on his tongue, but then she shifted her weight so that she could wrap her fingers around his rapidly swelling cock.

Given that double-barreled assault, he wouldn't last long. He had a hunch where she might be going with this routine. He wasn't opposed to letting her have her way with him at some point, but not right now.

He pulled back. "I think I know what you have in mind, and I—"

"It'll feel good." She gave him a teasing glance. "C'mon. Let me."

"I will, but not now."

"It could be an early birthday present."

"Or a belated one next time you come over." As he worked to dislodge her talented fingers, she resisted the effort.

Then she started giggling and it turned into a game. Soon he was laughing, too, and in serious danger of exploding. After finally prying her fingers loose, he got one arm under her tush and the other around her back. "This ends now."

"That's what you think."

"That's what I know, smarty-pants." Thank God for this huge bed. He had enough room to tumble her backwards onto the mattress and pin her down while he attempted to take control of the situation.

She wasn't about to let him and she was a champion wiggler. He had his hands full, plus he was running out of breath from laughing.

On top of that, he had to make sure he didn't accidentally hurt her or bend his cock out of shape. At least that was his excuse for why she won, rolling him to his back and straddling him.

Perched on his stomach, she braced her palms on his chest and flashed him a triumphant grin. "Gotcha."

"Yeah, you do." He sucked in air. "I need to up my game. Never wrestled with a farrier before."

"We're mighty."

"I agree."

"You know what, Montgomery?"

He smiled. Sounded good coming from her. "What, Zinnia?"

"Normally I'm not highly motivated to take a man's tallywacker in my mouth, but—"

"His what?"

"Tallywacker. You've never heard that before?"

He snorted. "No, ma'am."

"The point is, I want to do it now and you don't want me to. What's up with that? I thought it was the ultimate male fantasy."

"Oh, it is." The view from here was unbelievable. Luckily she'd granted him ogling privileges because he'd challenge any man to ignore her breasts as they dangled temptingly above him. But he wouldn't grab. "The thing is, I want to postpone that fantasy."

"Why on Earth would you want to do that?"

"Embarrassing as it is to admit, with you I seem to have the staying power of a gnat, and—"

"Do you know for a fact they're lousy in bed?"

"Not really."

"Then you shouldn't make assumptions. They may be small, but for all you know they're a rockin', sockin' *luuuv* machine." She did a little lap dance on his stomach.

"God almighty, Zinnia." He couldn't stop laughing. "I could come just looking at you." He'd never imagined this playful side of her. He was enchanted and so turned on he could hardly breathe.

"I think you have adequate staying power. You managed pretty well the first time around."

"That was in the good old missionary position. If you go down on me, I'll last about six seconds."

"So what?"

"I'd rather wait until I've built up some endurance so I can fully enjoy the experience." He also didn't want her giving him a blow job because she was feeling sorry for him after their name discussion. He wasn't crazy about telling her that.

"Hm. I see your point. So we'll stick with the missionary position until you get your mojo back?"

"Not necessarily. I kinda like where we ended up with our wrestling match." It would be a challenge, but he was willing to risk it.

"You're okay with me being on top?"

"Yep, especially if you'll let me play with your breasts in that scenario."

"You can play with them in any scenario. You've earned that right."

"Like now?"

"Except for now, because I have to pay a visit to the condom drawer. Be right back. Don't go away."

"I won't, but you should probably let me put it on."

"Are you kidding me right now?" She crawled to the drawer and opened it. "I can't wait to put this sucker on you. Surely you wouldn't deprive me of that special treat."

"You're killing me, lady."

"You'll love it."

"That's what I'm afraid of." And he had good reason.

When she came back, she brought him a pillow to prop under his head and she'd already taken the condom out of the package. Settling her sexy fanny on his thighs, she eyed his *tallywacker* with a gleam in her green eyes. Where had she heard that? He'd ask his brothers if they knew what it meant.

For the moment his job was making sure his tallywacker didn't turn into a geyser while she slowly rolled on the condom. He considered closing his eyes, but in the end he wanted to see even if it meant he ended up a hot mess.

Her technique was fine. Her pace was agonizingly slow. And there was that little smile of anticipation which drew his attention to her plump lips.

Was he a fool for not taking her up on her offer? So far he was surviving this routine, so he might have sailed through it like a stud. Then she cupped his balls. He gasped and clenched his jaw, holding back the orgasm that almost was.

She glanced up. "Like that?"

"You bet." He sounded like he'd swallowed a mouthful of gravel. "Now please let go."

"*O*-kay." She gave a little bounce to the first syllable. Rising to her knees, she crawled forward, her gaze locked with his.

No doubt about it, she was on the prowl. And she was coming for him. He swallowed. *Next time, let's close the windows.* That had been her suggestion, not his. He'd done her bidding and clearly she planned to make him yell.

It was hardly the first time he'd made love this way, but it was his first time with Zinnia. Her physicality had transfixed him the instant she'd stepped out of Graham's truck.

He hadn't acknowledged that he wanted a woman who'd wrestle with him and hold her own. But his body had known. When she'd appeared, an instinct deep within him had whispered *this one.*

He'd bought the biggest bed he could find, one that required special-order sheets. Finally he knew why he'd insisted on having all this space. For Zinnia.

Laying her palms on his chest just under his collarbone, she kept her tush in the air as she bent her elbows until her nipples brushed back and forth against his. "Feel that?"

"Sure do. Are we giving off sparks?"

"Not yet. Soon. You're free to touch my girls whenever they're in range."

"Thanks."

"Like now."

"You want me to?"

"I do." She dipped her head and nibbled on his mouth. "They like it."

Taking a breath, he gathered paradise into his hands, letting the weight rest in his palms while he brushed his thumbs lazily over her nipples.

As they stiffened, she moaned softly and rocked forward, offering a gift to his waiting mouth. He didn't take that gesture lightly. He'd bet she'd never made it before.

And he treated it like the privilege it was, loving her with all his might until her cries grew breathless and her body began to shake.

"I need you."

Her low-pitched, husky admission sent fire shooting through his veins. "Take what you want."

Pushing away, she slid her hands to his abs and lowered her hips. "Help me."

He grasped his cock and guided it into place, his heart going a million miles an hour.

She didn't waste any time. In one quick motion, she yelled yee-*haw* and took him up to the hilt. He laughed at that, but the intense connection stole his breath, turning his pithy swear word into a murmur.

Then she started moving and holy hell. Needing something to hold, he grabbed her hips as he met each downward stroke with an upward thrust.

She gave him the ride of a lifetime, one that ended too soon in a noisy and jubilant mutual climax. Panting, welded to her in what felt like an unbreakable bond, he stared into her wide eyes. His were likely the same.

She gulped for air. "What just happened?"

"Wild monkey sex?"

She nodded slowly. "I'd buy that." She took another deep breath. "I've never yelled *yee-haw* in my life."

"You mean during sex?"

"I mean during anything. That phrase has never come out of my mouth before."

He grinned. "I liked it. Seemed to fit the moment."

"Let's keep it to ourselves."

"As I understand it, we're keeping all of this to ourselves."

"Except for Mari. I won't tell her I yelled *yee-haw.*"

"Why not? It's kinda funny. You'd make her laugh."

"I would, but then she'd... never mind. I'm not telling her."

"If that's settled, I have to make a little trip."

"Oh, right." She disengaged with care and flopped back on the bed.

He climbed out on shaky legs, as if he'd just been tossed around by the biggest coaster in the amusement park. Cleaning up quickly, he returned to the bed. "Need anything?"

"A cuddle."

"I gots you." He gathered her close and let out a sigh. The next thing he knew it was morning. And Zinnia was gone.

22

Zinnia would have loved to drift off to sleep with Monty, but she'd resisted the urge. Once he'd conked out, she'd left the bed, pulled on her pjs, located her flip-flops and tip-toed out of the room.

She'd found a pad and pen in the kitchen and written him a note thanking him for a lovely evening, wishing him a happy birthday, and letting him know her sister had Sunday night off. She'd signed the note with an XO, the middle ground between *sincerely* and *love.*

She'd been jubilant on the way back to the house, but creeping inside had given her a mild case of guilt. Despite that, she'd fallen gratefully into bed, half asleep as her head hit the pillow. If nothing else, she and Monty would temporarily cure each other's insomnia on the nights they spent together.

The minute the alarm on her phone chimed the next morning, Tex barreled into her room, eyes shining with excitement. "You gots to get up, Mommy! We gots to get ready!"

"The party starts at four this afternoon, sweetie." She sat up.

"How long before we gots to go, Mommy?"

She gazed into that innocent little face. Her mild sense of guilt from last night had been replaced with guilt that had the kick of a mule.

She picked up her phone from the nightstand and turned it toward him. "What time is it now?"

"Six-o-five."

Her son had talked endlessly about the party at dinner last night. He'd been incandescent with joy at the prospect of seeing his idol today and giving him a birthday present.

"Then let's count the hours." She held up her hand. "Count with me. Seven, eight, nine, ten, eleven. How many hours is that?"

He consulted his spread fingers. "Five."

Switching hands, she continued the countdown. "Twelve, one, two, three, four. How many hours is that?"

He groaned. "Five *again*. Can we go early? Mister Monty wants to see me. I know he does."

"I'm sure he does, but if we go early, they won't be ready for us. They'll still be setting up."

"We could help!"

"Not this time, sweetie. We're just getting to know the Bridgers, and—"

"Where's my wrangler?" Uncle Graham's voice drifted down the hall. "Time to feed the herd, buddy!"

"Yes, sir!" Tex glanced down at his pjs. "Uh-oh. I gots to get dressed. You too, Mommy!"

"I'll be ready in a flash."

"Me, too!" He raced back to his bedroom.

She hurried through a quick sponge bath before throwing on some clothes. She'd be the last one down to the barn, but that was fine. No client appointments today.

Some coffee would be nice, too. Mari would have made a pot and left her some. The whir of an electric mixer told her two things — waffles were on the breakfast menu and her sis had lingered in the kitchen to get the 411 on last night. Made her smile.

When they'd lived in Great Falls, they'd divided the chores. Mari had done most of the cooking and Zinnia had handled the bulk of the cleaning. They'd continued the system here. Relieving their uncle of that work was the least they could do to thank him for taking them in.

Mari shut off the mixer when she walked in. "Hey, there."

"Hey." She grabbed a mug, poured herself some coffee and pretended not to know why Mari was still in the house. "You're going down to the barn, right?"

"Absolutely. I can't wait to see that cutie-pie. I just wanted to mix the batter first, so we're ready to roll when we all come back in."

"Then making the batter has *nothing* to do with you itching to find out how things went last night?"

She laughed. "You know me too well."

"And you know me too well. You were right about this matchup. It was awesome. He's awesome."

"Woo-hoo!" Mari spun away from the counter and rushed over to give her a hug.

"Watch the coffee, watch the coffee."

"I am." Her sis gave her a quick squeeze and stepped back. "I'm just happy for you. I assume you're going back tomorrow night?"

"Probably, although we didn't confirm it and I snuck out while he was asleep. I left him a note, though, so he's aware you're not working Sunday night."

"He fell asleep?" Returning to the mixer, she dropped the beaters in the sink. "That surprises me."

"I almost did, but I decided to leave and make sure I'd get back in plenty of time. Besides, we both needed sleep. He's an insomniac, too."

"What you just said makes no sense." She tucked the batter in the fridge. "Two insomniacs should be up all night doing it like bunnies."

"Well, it appears that good sex is a cure."

"I'll be damned." Mari picked up a half-full mug from the counter and raised it in her direction. "See? You were made for each other."

"Mm." Avoiding her sister's gaze, she sipped her coffee.

"What's wrong?"

"I told myself I wasn't taking anything away from Tex by going over there, but—"

"You're not. He's asleep and you're doing something for yourself for a change. And curing your insomnia in the process. Win-win."

"If it's win-win, why do I feel so rotten about sneaking off to spend hours alone with the cowboy he idolizes? Why do I cringe at the thought of him finding out? He would feel betrayed."

"He won't find out. Besides, you don't want him spending a lot of time with Mister Monty, remember? You're afraid he'll get too attached."

"I know, but when he came into my room this morning all bubbly and eager to go over there today, and I'd just had a wonderful couple of hours with the guy...."

"Zinnia Dawn." Setting down her mug, Mari took her by the shoulders. "You and Tex are two separate people. You need closeness with Monty and Tex needs some daylight."

"But—"

"You can nobly sacrifice your needs if you must, but that won't help Tex wean himself away from Mister Monty. Only time can do that."

She gazed at her little sis. "You're right. Again."

"Of course I am."

"I hope you know you're flipping the script. I'm supposed to be the wise older sister giving you advice."

"Don't worry. The script will flip again one of these days." She smiled. "C'mon. Let's go see how many layers of cuteness that little guy has added since last night."

"Yeah, let's do that." As they walked down to the barn, Zinnia vowed to spend the next several hours focused on her son, her mare, and the new baby.

She failed miserably. Tex kept bringing up Mister Monty and the impending party. On top of it, Speckles' adorable foal was his namesake. By the time she settled Tex in his car seat and climbed into the passenger side of Uncle Graham's fancy red truck, her excitement about seeing that cowboy again rivaled her son's.

They didn't live far away, and when Tex got a load of the imposing metal gate decorated with a running horse, his eyes widened. When they drove through and her uncle announced they were now on ranch property, her son went supernova.

"All this?" He spread his arms wide. "All this is Mister Monty's?"

"Not just his." She turned from the passenger seat to look at him fully. His car seat was helpful since the elevation gave him a better view. "It belongs to his whole family."

"Look at all the trees! They have so many trees!"

"They do."

"Mommy, Mommy!" He pointed to his right. "I seed a horse over there. And another one! They're loose!"

"They're wild, buddy," Uncle Graham said. "But they're not loose. There's a fence. You just can't see it very well because it blends into the trees."

He gasped. "They're *wild*? Like in *The Black Stallion*?"

She nodded. "Like that." A couple months ago she'd decided he was old enough to watch the movie, and he'd loved it, even if the boy in it wasn't strictly speaking a cowboy.

"Whoa. Why do they gots wild horses?"

"They rescued them."

"Why?"

"To keep them safe." It was more complex than that. Uncle Graham had told her that horses, though beautiful, weren't native to Montana. They created issues for native grazers like deer and antelope. The Hearts and Hooves Sanctuary provided an elegant solution.

"Safe from bears?"

"Yes." The fence likely kept out bears. After they'd moved here, she'd done her best to warn him about wild creatures without making them sound so scary he'd be afraid to go outside.

"Smokey wouldn't eat a horse."

"Because he's a tame bear."

"Yep." His attention shifted as they approached the turn-off to the ranch. "*Another* gate?"

"This is the last one, buddy." Uncle Graham braked beside the keypad and punched in the code. "Once we get around that bend, you'll be able to see the ranch."

"Ohboyohboyohboy." He bounced in his seat. "I've been waiting *forever.*"

She felt like bouncing in her seat, too. Around that bend a certain cowboy was watching for her.

Surrounded by his loving family, he'd be laughing and talking with everyone, maybe wearing a new shirt someone had bought for him, maybe sipping a beer. But he'd be keeping his eye on the road.

Her stomach quivered. Mari's words hadn't banished her guilt. It was still there, especially whenever she glanced at Tex.

But she knew one thing for sure. Guilt wouldn't stop her from driving back over here on Sunday night.

23

"Watching for someone?"

Monty turned to find his mom walking toward him wearing her *I know what you're thinking* smile.

"Yes, ma'am. Graham should be here any minute. I can't wait to see Tex's face when he first sees the Beaver Bunch." He glanced toward the circular platform where the barn's hayloft used to be. A jug band made up of three life-sized animatronic beavers sat there now thanks to his brother-in-law Cole's ingenuity.

"He'll love it. So will Zinnia."

"Definitely." Dear God, he hoped he wasn't blushing. Felt like he was, though. "But I was mostly thinking of Tex." *Liar, liar, pants on fire.*

"She's a lovely woman."

Oh, yeah, his mom had his number. She'd probably caught all his tells. "And she has a good sense of humor." That sounded platonic, right? Like he totally hadn't slept with her?

"I'm glad you invited her today."

"And Graham. It'll be good to see him when he doesn't have work to—"

"Hey, birthday boy!" Claudie called out. "Are you on this team or not?"

"I am, I am." He made his way back to the horseshoe pit. "Just checking on the coals." He'd walked over near the fire pit to get away from the noise of the horseshoe tournament so he could listen for the distinctive rumble of Graham's truck.

"The coals are not your job," Adam sang out. "No working on your b-day." He and Tracy were still busy tying birthday balloons everywhere. Evidently they'd bought a truckload of the things.

"Seems to me you were staring into space." Rio punched him playfully on the shoulder. "I guess that happens when you get old."

"No fair teasing him on his birthday." Greta, the most tender-hearted of the Bridger Bunch, came over and gave him a hug.

Claudie snorted. "That's the perfect time. Step up to the plate, little brother. Shockingly, we're behind. Make us proud."

By *us*, she meant a foursome comprised of Claudie, him, Auntie Kat and Auntie Ezzie. Greta, Rio, Grandma Doris and Auntie Carmen made up the opposing team.

The Dazzling Damsels all had good arms. They'd even created a horseshoe pit behind the bunkhouse so they could work on their game.

Their setup might be in better shape than the family one situated in an informal picnic area to the left of the ranch house. In winter this yard was where they staged snowball fights, built forts, and snow families.

In the summer they resurrected the horseshoe pit and hauled the wooden picnic tables out of the tractor barn. The fire pit, set a distance away so random sparks wouldn't catch the tables on fire, was spruced up by cementing in the stones that had fallen out during a heavy freeze.

He picked up a horseshoe and took his position.

"Hang on a minute, Monty." Auntie Kat sauntered over. The top of her head barely reached his shoulder, yet she'd forged a successful modeling career despite being short. "It looks like you've abandoned that floating arm trick I showed you last summer."

"You're so right. I completely forgot." He'd had Zinnia brain since last night. It was his only excuse and he couldn't use it.

"Then let me refresh your memory. You do this." Picking up a horseshoe, she flattened her palm, stiffened her arm and brought it to shoulder height. "Keep your arm straight. No wavering. Swing your arm back down, swing it back up and let that sucker fly."

"I remember now. Thanks." Once she'd focused his attention on the game, his brain clicked into gear. He'd been the only one of his siblings who'd adopted Auntie Kat's new delivery last summer. The Damsels, aka his aunties and grandma, had been using it since this game started.

That he'd failed to notice showed how rattled he was. Why had he thought he could pull off this secrecy thing?

Gripping a horseshoe, he flattened his palm, stiffened his arm and brought it to shoulder height. Then he let it swing down and centrifugal force brought it back up.

She's here. The growl of Graham's truck torpedoed his concentration and delivered a hefty dose of adrenaline. As it poured through his system, he couldn't seem to let go of the horseshoe.

When he finally did, way too high in the arc, it sailed over the stake and keep going. The four people standing there scattered. It finally landed a couple of yards beyond the stake.

Rio let out a whistle. "What the hell was *that*?"

Shaken by the burst of energy, he gazed at the spot where the horseshoe rested. "I don't know what happened. It was like the horseshoe was glued to my hand." And Zinnia was in that truck. Her energy tugged at him but he needed to stay put.

Rio put his fist to his mouth and mimicked a carnival barker. "And for his next trick, Monty Bridger will lift a car!"

"Hilarious, bro." Funny, but in that moment, he might've been able to do it. "Who's up next?"

"Me." Auntie Ezzie, even shorter than Auntie Kat, danced up to the plate. "You know what we need? Walk-up songs. We should each have a walk-up song."

"Tell me what you want," Rio said. "Greta and I will sing it."

Greta laughed. "Yeah, we will. Loud, too."

"Bueno! Sing *Beer Never Broke My Heart.* I'll back away and come back in."

Monty gave thanks for the distraction provided by his quirky family as he struggled to keep his attention on the game. Rio and Greta belted out the first few bars of the Luke Combs tune while Auntie Ezzie pranced up to the plate. She got a ringer, so now all the Damsels wanted a walk-up song.

So damn cute. If he could just focus on—

"Mister Monty, Mister Monty!" He spun around and here came Tex, legs and arms pumping, his cowboy hat bouncing against his back, the string around his neck keeping it from falling.

Zinnia was a couple of yards behind him, calling his name and gaining fast. The little kid must have gotten a head start. No way could he outrun her.

He was halfway to the horseshoe pit when she caught him and scooped him up in her arms. He immediately started pleading for his freedom while Zinnia tried to talk him down.

What to do? It really wasn't a question. He glanced at his teammates. "I gotta—"

"Go, go." Claudie waved her hands in Zinnia's direction. "Poor kid looks like he's ready to cry."

Sure enough, by the time he arrived, Tex had tears dribbling down his face.

"Hey, sport." He pulled a bandanna from his back pocket and gave it to him. "Looks like you could use this."

He scrubbed his face. "I'm not s'posed to run over there, but I seed you, and…." He sniffed, blew his nose on the bandanna and handed it back.

Wadding it up, he returned it to his back pocket. "And here I am." His throat was tight and something funky was going on with his heart.

"My apologies."

Zinnia's soft voice caused him to look at her for the first time. He'd been so wrapped up in

Tex's misery he'd ignored the woman who'd occupied his thoughts all day. That was startling.

The anxiety in her green eyes wasn't good news. She didn't want Tex getting attached and he'd just demonstrated he was extremely attached.

He cleared his throat. "It's fine."

"I didn't realize he'd take off like that. I guess I should have. You were in the middle of a game, weren't you?"

"No problem. I'd just taken my turn."

"We gots you a present."

"Thank you, sport. That was very generous."

"Mommy wrapped it but I put on the tape."

"I can't wait to see what it is."

"We gots it in the truck. But you gots to wait."

"I know. We usually—"

"Hey, you guys." His mom arrived with Graham. "Graham and I had an idea. We just talked the horseshoe players into pausing the game so Cole can do his thing." She glanced at him. "We'll repeat it later, of course, since it's very cool to see when it's dark, but Tex and Zinnia have never seen it, so why not go ahead and enjoy it now?"

"Good plan." Family to the rescue.

Or family as matchmakers? Were they putting it all together now that they had eyes on Zinnia and her son? He hadn't figured out the optics of this situation until this very minute.

Everyone at the party lived on the ranch except for Tracy's parents, who'd driven over from their place bordering Laughing Creek. It was a big group but a tight group. That gave his invitation to Zinnia and Tex significance.

And now they'd all seen Zinnia. Stunning Zinnia. And her adorable kid, who clearly idolized him. They couldn't be blamed for jumping to conclusions.

Because of his thoughtless gesture, Zinnia and Tex were smack-dab in the bosom of his family. The Bridger Bunch would fall in love with these two and make assumptions about his intentions.

What had he done?

24

What had she done? When Zinnia had accepted Monty's birthday party invitation two days ago… had it only been two days ago? Sadly, yes. How little time it took to turn her life and Tex's upside down.

She'd accepted because she'd known her cowboy-obsessed son would love it here. Experiencing this gorgeous ranch would be the equivalent of Disneyland for him.

And it was. So many cowboys, so many horses grazing in the pasture. A ranch house with a long front porch and rocking chairs just like in the movies. A barn right out of the movies, too.

While Monty's brother-in-law Cole headed up to the apartment above it so he could set up the Beaver Bunch show, Monty introduced her and Tex to the rest of the family. And they were all family at this party.

Somehow she'd missed that she, Tex and Uncle Graham would be the only people here who weren't connected to the Bridgers by blood or marriage. This wasn't just a birthday party. It was a family gathering.

He'd invited her on impulse driven by lust. She hadn't cared about his motives if it meant Tex could come along. Two days later, she was on a runaway horse. She'd lost control of the narrative.

Clearly his family had decided she and Monty were a couple. Some already knew about the foaling but others were just finding out that Monty had spent the night in Uncle Graham's barn.

If they asked for more detail, Tex was more than willing to give it, including what he'd named the foal who was officially his. Why hadn't she seen all this coming?

All the smiles and laughter told her they were on board with this romance even if it had come out of the blue. She and Tex were more than welcome to join the Bridger Bunch.

Monty was all smiles and laughter, too, but she knew him better now. He was as uncomfortable as she was. Maybe more. They needed to talk, but how? When?

Picnic benches were lined up in front of the barn and everyone was finding a seat. They insisted she and Tex sit up front, and with Monty of course. Uncle Graham also scored a front row seat because he'd only seen the show once.

Someone, she thought it was Monty's older brother Zay, suggested Monty put Tex on his shoulders so he could see better. When he swung Tex up there and he gave a little whoop of joy, it made her throat hurt.

He was mesmerized by those little critters, each one wearing a kid-sized cowboy hat like his. "They gots cowboy hats like mine, Mommy."

"I see that. Pretty cute."

"When are they gonna start?"

"Any minute, sport."

"Howdy, ladies and gents!" Cole altered his voice to sound more folksy. "Presenting the Beaver Bunch!"

The group clapped and cheered. So did Tex, bouncing and clapping so enthusiastically that Monty had to grab his legs so he didn't topple off.

"That's Rufus on the fiddle, Buster's on the washboard and Shorty's on the washtub bass. Rufus, want to say a few words?"

The fiddle player's mouth moved and Cole's drawl got more pronounced. "Shore do, boss! I'd like to welcome all these good folks to our show and give a shout-out to our special guests Tex and Zinnia!"

More clapping from everyone except Tex, who sat stunned. "Mommy, he knowed our names!"

"Must be a smart little beaver."

"Got a song for us, Rufus?"

"Shore do, boss. Let's do it, boys!" Slapping their tails in time to the music, their paws manipulating those instruments, they played *The Gambler.*

"Mommy! It's our song!"

"I know, son." She glanced at Monty, eyebrows raised.

He lowered his voice. "He asked. And he happened to have it."

She had no words. He'd listened to her unconventional lullaby and then remembered it when Cole asked for a favorite song. Was he trying to make her fall in love with him?

"C'mon folks!" Rufus called out. "Join in on the chorus! Y'all know the words!"

The concert turned into a singalong, and nobody sang with more gusto than her beloved son. The crowd began to sway with the music. Uncle Graham on her left and Monty on her right swayed, so she could either go along or get bumped.

Once she was in motion and singing, something unexpected happened to her anxiety. It disappeared. Or maybe it was the words of the song. Advice to live by.

She certainly was sitting at the table right now, and the dealing was far from done. Tex was having the time of his life. Maybe she should just keep playing the game and see if her hand improved.

25

It was the damnedest thing. Monty wasn't surprised that Tex was such a hit with his family. Zinnia was, too, but Tex was in demand and he lapped up the attention.

Monty was glad for the kid. He really was. He was also jealous as hell. While Tex didn't exactly ignore him, he was mostly busy talking to Monty's brothers and Cole, the magician in charge of the Beaver Bunch.

Adam gave Tex a tour of the barn. Luis showed him the other barn, the one for the semi-wild horses being trained for adoption. Zay took him for a ride on the new John Deere Gator the ranch had just purchased for checking the water tanks in the sanctuary.

Rio even searched the attic for a toy set of horseshoes and everyone took turns playing with Tex. Monty did, too, but it wasn't like the kid was more excited to play with him than anyone else.

To be hurt because he wasn't Tex's main man anymore was jacked up and he knew it. If the family in general took an interest in that little boy it would gradually loosen the bonds between them.

He should want that since he'd been as worried about Tex getting overly attached as Zinnia was. She was probably thrilled with the turn of events. He would be, too, once he got his head on straight.

When it was time for dinner, everybody wanted to sit with Tex. As Monty was filling his plate, Zinnia walked over, a bemused smile on her face. "He really doesn't need me. Want to sit together?"

"Sure. He doesn't need me, either."

"A steady diet of this wouldn't be good, but I guess one afternoon and evening won't ruin him for life."

"Hey, birthday boy, over here." Luis beckoned to him from the table he and Jordan shared with Mila and Cole. "We saved a spot for you and Zinnia."

"Appreciate it." He glanced at Zinnia.

"Sounds great."

The women occupied one side and the men the other. He slid in next to Luis and Zinnia sat next to Jordan.

Luis motioned to the table where Tex was holding court with their mom, Graham and the Damsels. "Looks like you've been upstaged, little brother."

"No worries. He's having a ball."

"I'm getting a preview of what it'll be like when Liberty's born next month." Jordan laid her hand on her large belly. "I hope somebody else gets preggers soon or Liberty's gonna be spoiled rotten."

"I hear you," Zinnia said. "Tex will be bored out of his gourd tomorrow with a measly audience of me, my sister and my uncle."

"I'm sorry she couldn't make it." Mila leaned around Jordan. "Mom said she's working at the Raccoon tonight."

"She is or she would have loved to come. It was kind of your mom to invite all of us."

Monty's breath caught. She'd just shifted the blame — or credit? — for the invitation to his mother. Nicely done.

"I'm glad she did," Cole said. "Having a kid in the audience was fun. We need more kids around here."

"Hey, big brother. Does that mean I can count on you and Mila to provide the next addition to the Bridger Bunch?"

He smiled. "Maybe, Jordie. Maybe."

Jordan's attention snapped to Mila. "Are you—"

"Maybe." Mila's dark eyes sparkled. "But it's too soon to—"

"Ohmigosh!" She gave Mila a sideways hug. "I won't say a word, I promise. But that would be so cool."

"Hang on." Zinnia looked at Jordan. "Cole is your brother?"

"Yep. Without me, Mila and Cole never would have met. When I showed up here last July I had no idea I was about to change both my life and his."

"That sounds like a good story."

"Two good stories." Luis took a sip of his beer. "Monty was part of the drama. Jordie needed a vet on short notice for Fudge, who had an abscess. I coaxed her to trailer him down from Missoula so Monty could take care of him."

"Monty to the rescue." Zinnia gave him a wink.

"He became sort of an unintentional cupid," Luis said. "Fudge had to stay so Monty could treat him, so naturally she had to stay at the ranch, too."

"I'll admit sometimes I was an intentional cupid. I could see you two belong together."

Jordan smiled. "Thanks for that, Monty. Took us a while to figure it out. Anyway, once I was staying on the ranch I got permission to invite my brother, and the rest is history."

"Uncle Graham told me about your fabulous training center and Luis's work with wild horses. Mila, you run the Hearts and Hooves adoption program, right?"

"It's me and Claudie. I handle the adoptions and she does the marketing."

Zinnia nodded. "Makes sense that program needs two people. I'm gradually getting it all straight. Cole, what about you?"

"Oh, I just play with animatronics."

"I doubt that."

"He's the head of ranch maintenance," Mila said. "It's a huge job. We didn't realize how huge because my dad just quietly did everything."

"So I've heard." She looked across the table, her gaze holding his. "An amazing person."

"Which means I have big shoes to fill," Cole said. "Luckily the Bridger Bunch is pretty handy. I count on that help when things get too crazy."

"I can see it's a big operation." Zinnia turned to Jordan. "Since your specialty is training, I'd love to hire you for a consultation as I get into this adventure with Tex and his foal. I want them to grow and learn together, but I have no idea what I'm doing."

"Just one consultation? I'd be glad to do more. Of course baby Liberty will change my schedule, but I plan to keep working."

"I wish I could say yes to that, but I doubt I can afford it."

"You'd get the family rate."

"But I'm not—"

"Close enough." She glanced at Monty. "Am I right?"

He gulped. "Um…"

"Oh, geez, me and my big mouth. Blame it on pregnancy brain. This thing is brand new and I'm an idiot. Forgive me for putting you on the spot. Forget I said that, please. Zinnia, we'll talk. I'm sure we can work something out."

"I'm sure we can."

He sucked in air. So much for diffusing the bomb by making it sound like his mother had orchestrated Zinnia's presence here. He might as well own this fustercluck.

After dinner came the cakes, plural. His mom had long ago given up the idea of one cake. It would have to be rolled in on a wheelbarrow.

And after the candle-blowing routine, which was always a challenge for outdoor birthdays like his, everyone settled in with cake and ice cream. When everyone was almost done, he announced he'd start opening presents.

That brought Tex right over to the table that had been designated for it. "Can I help, Mister Monty?"

Zinnia put a hand on his shoulder. "Come sit by me, son. Opening presents is for the person having the birthday."

"Oh." The light disappeared from his eyes. "Okay, Mommy."

The disappointment on that previously smiling little face got to him. "Your mom's right, sport. Normally I'd do this all by myself since it's my birthday and these are my presents. But I'm kinda tired from all the fun we've been having. I could use a little help, if you're available."

"I am! Can I, Mommy?"

"You can, but you're not allowed to rip the paper. Be very careful. Sometimes people like to save the wrapping paper."

"I will! I'll be *so* careful!"

"Oh, I don't—" He shut his trap when he got a look from Zinnia. "I just don't understand why more people don't save paper. I'm way into saving paper." He ignored the snort from Rio.

He paid for caving to the little guy's disappointed face. They all did. Unwrapping the gifts took freaking forever. Fortunately some came in bags. Even then, Tex insisted on folding the tissue paper.

Greta came around with two big pitchers of beer. Thirty minutes later she came around again. Several times Rio hummed the theme song from *Jeopardy* under his breath, but he also called out words of encouragement along with everyone else.

Despite the slow pace of the endeavor, Tex was winning hearts and minds with his dedication to the cause.

"I think we've got us a future wild horse trainer," Luis called out. "Don't often see that kind of patience."

"Or he could be a baker," Greta said. "Attention to detail is important for baking."

Tex glanced up. "I'm gonna be a cowboy."

"You could be a cowboy *and* a baker."

"Yep. I maded some brownies with Auntie Mari." As the Damsels let out a communal sigh of pure love, Tex went back to slowly peeling tape away from the next wrapped gift.

Eventually only one was left, wrapped in cowboy-themed paper that reminded him of Tex's pjs. He had a hunch that paper had made an appearance when Tex had his fifth birthday.

Tex had pushed it aside each time Monty reached for another present, muttering *we gots to save it for last.* Where had he learned that the best gift should be opened last?

"Well, sport, I guess this is it. Ready to open it for me?"

He shook his head and grinned. "You gots to open it. Mommy tolded me you'll like it. You'll really, *really* like it."

"I'm sure I will." He could tell it was a book. He'd been holding off buying Rance McLintock's latest thinking someone would get it for him, likely his mom. She might have put the bug in Graham's ear. Or Zinnia's.

"You put a lot of tape on here, Tex."

"I like tape."

"You do a good job with it. A thorough job."

"I know." He crowded up against him, quivering with eagerness.

Finally he peeled off the last bit of tape and pulled the paper away. "Awesome! It's *A Bullet Through the Beer Keg*! I really wanted this one!"

"I know!" Tex hopped up and down. "We gots you it — me, Mommy and Uncle G!"

"Thank you. Thank you so much."

"You're welcome." Tex grabbed him around the waist and looked up, his eyes shining. "Happy birthday, Mister Monty."

Damned if he didn't get all emotional. He had to clear his throat before he could say *thank you* again. Around him others were doing the same.

His whole family had fallen in love with Tex. And so had he.

Which meant he needed to distance himself from this adorable kid. And his even more adorable mother.

26

This was getting out of hand. Zinnia needed to talk with Monty. At the outset of this party she'd figured they wouldn't spend much time together to avoid giving the wrong impression.

But Tex had immediately blown her cover and Monty's family was convinced they were a couple about to create a little family of three. Monty didn't want that. She didn't want that. Or so she told herself.

Falling in love and making a commitment to a guy she'd just met would be irresponsible even if she didn't have Tex to consider. Throw that little sweetie into the mix and she'd be forsaking her duty as a mother.

She was clear on those points. She wasn't clear on what Monty was thinking. He kept choosing paths that tightened the connection between him and Tex.

He'd figured out a way for Tex to sleep in the barn the night of the foaling. He'd set up the bucket routine so her son could be the first member of the family to interact with that baby.

Then today he'd been put out that Tex spent so much time with his brothers. He hadn't said so, but she could tell from his expression. Just now he'd allowed Tex to unwrap all the birthday presents.

His decisions didn't match his claim that he wasn't ready to be a father figure. Then again, hers didn't line up with her comments, either.

Knowing he had the hots for her, she'd still accepted his birthday party invitation. Now she was sleeping with him when she'd sworn to stay away from men until Tex was older. Way older.

As light faded from the sky, Tex started yawning. While he was distracted by Ezzie performing the cha-cha, she got her uncle aside. "We should think about leaving soon, before he gets overtired."

"Gotcha. Let me ask when Cole's doing the night version of the Beaver Bunch. It's worth seeing, and we can leave right after."

"Good plan." As her uncle went in search of Cole, she scanned the group and spotted Monty. Ezzie was now teaching the cha-cha to Tex. She hurried over to Monty. "Can I talk to you for a minute?"

"Yes, ma'am. I've been meaning to talk to you. Let's walk out toward the pasture. Nobody's over there."

"That works."

When they were several yards from the crowd, he stopped. "This should do it. Are you fixing to take Tex home? I caught him yawning."

"Yes, but I wanted to let you know that I…I don't think we should keep seeing each other."

"I don't either."

"Really?" She gazed at him. He'd had a great time last night. He had more self-control than she'd given him credit for. This would be easier than she'd thought. "Good. That's good. We're on the same page."

"But I think we deserve one more night before we call it quits."

That lit the fire that she'd kept subdued ever since arriving here. *One more night.* Then she thought of something. "Is this because you didn't get to enjoy—"

"No, that's not it." He chuckled. "I forgot about that, but now that you mention it…."

"Cut it out. I don't want to go back to the party all hot and bothered."

"Too late for me. I've been hot and bothered ever since you suggested this talk."

"That's the main reason we have to stop seeing each other. Your family thinks we're an item and it's hard to deny it with a straight face when we're having wild monkey sex every few nights."

"They have a spidey sense when it comes to relationships. They can tell we're into each other."

"Well, we've gotta put a lid on it, for everyone's sake."

"Especially Tex's." He rubbed the back of his neck. "I love that little guy, but if I'm not planning to become a significant part of his life, I need to back the hell off."

"Wow. I was just going to tell you that. Thanks for figuring it out."

"I realized today that if you and Tex pop over to the ranch now and then, he'll get his cowboy fix through my brothers. Everyone took a shine to him. He doesn't need me."

The sadness in his voice tugged at her heart. "I doubt he'll throw you over that quickly."

"Oh, he won't, but if I quit... I don't know, just...."

"Looking for ways to make him happy?"

"Yeah, exactly. I love seeing his eyes light up. He's such a cool kid, with his brownie-serving routine, and his Smokey Bear, and obsession with tape. Oh, my God, the tape! Do you buy it by the gross or what?"

"We go through quite a bit of tape." Did Monty know he sounded like a proud father? A loving father?

But for some reason, he didn't want that role. She had a hunch there was more to it than not being ready because he was only twenty-seven.

He took a quick breath. "Okay. I've made my pitch for spending one more night together, but I don't recall you giving a thumbs-up or thumbs-down. Which is it?"

She stuck her hand in front of his face.

"Ah, Zinnia." He wrapped his hands around her fist and kissed her upraised thumb. "I'm gonna miss you."

"I'll miss you, too, but neither one of us wants to risk making a big mistake, especially with Tex involved."

"That's the crux of it."

"Hey, lovebirds!" Rio called out. "We're doing the Beaver Bunch thing in five minutes! Be there or be square!"

She giggled. "Be there or be square? Where did he learn that?"

"Auntie Kat. Those two are super close." He squeezed her hand and let go. "He lives in her Swiss chalet and she has all sorts of fifties and sixties stuff on display in there. He left it up."

"You live in your grandmother's cottage. I'll bet you're super close with her."

"I am. In fact, after what she's seen tonight, I'll bet she'll pay me a visit tomorrow to find out what's going on. Chances are she and my mom have already found a moment to discuss it. Grandma Doris is the logical one to grill me."

"What are you going to tell her?"

"I'm not gonna spill the tea about the monkey sex, if that's what you're worried about."

"I wasn't. Well, maybe a little."

"Even though she's very open-minded, I don't feel the need to talk about my sex life with her. I will tell her that we have amazing chemistry, but I'm not ready for fatherhood and even if I were, you're not crazy about committing to a man you barely know. So we're backing away before Tex gets any more invested."

"I couldn't have said it better. I might steal that for when I talk to Uncle—"

"Hey, guys, not kidding! Get over here or you'll miss it!"

He nudged back the brim of his hat. "We need to go."

"We do."

"See you tomorrow night." He leaned in and gave her a butterfly kiss on the mouth.

The unexpected kiss immobilized her for a second and she had to walk fast to catch up with his long strides. "What was that?"

"I don't know. I just had to." He kept walking.

"Why?"

"I wanted to send a message. Couldn't stay, though, or I would've done it again."

"What message?"

"That I care about you." He stared straight ahead. "That I want you to be happy. That I wish things were different."

Those words ran on a loop in her head during the Beaver Bunch performance. They sat in the same place, and Monty let Tex climb up on his shoulders again so he could see better.

The show was even more magical at night. Footlights and beaver-sized red hanging lanterns made the knotty pine backdrop glow like warm honey.

The Beaver Bunch played two songs this time, tunes Cole had obviously geared toward Tex. First came Gene Autry's *Back in the Saddle Again* followed by the Roy Rogers and Dale Evens' classic *Happy Trails.*

Tex knew them both from watching old TV shows. Like last time, Rufus invited everyone to join in on the chorus. She swayed with the crowd, her shoulder moving in tandem with Monty's, their hips nestled against each other.

She likely wouldn't experience another moment like this. If the Bridgers operated like most families, Monty's explanation to his grandma would make its way around until everyone had heard it.

He might get some questions, even pushback from his siblings, but if he stuck to the script, they'd probably drop the subject. The faux romance would be over. She and Tex wouldn't repeat this cozy togetherness with Monty ever again.

It was for the best, but it made her sad. He'd said he wanted her to be happy. But clearly he didn't see himself as part of that scenario. If he had, then maybe, over time....

But he'd been very clear. No point in dwelling on what could never be.

27

Monty sure had called it. When his grandma hugged him goodnight, she asked if she could pop over for a cup of coffee sometime. He had the next day relatively free since it was Sunday, so he suggested ten in the morning. Luckily he still had sticky buns.

She arrived promptly and asked if they could sit on the front porch.

"Absolutely. It's beautiful out there."

"That's not the only reason I asked. I told everybody I'm gonna find out what the heck is going on. If they see us sitting on your porch they'll know I'll have the scoop. They won't need to pester you."

"I see." He set the tray loaded with two mugs, a carafe and a plate of sticky buns on the small wooden table between the two rockers.

"I always loved that tray. Rustic, yet elegant."

"I use it all the time. Thanks for leaving it for me."

"We're chock-a-block with trays at the Dorm. Ezzie and Carmen have ones from Mexico and Kat has ones from Paris, Rome, Switzerland, you name it. She was a traveling fool."

He smiled at the description of his feisty Auntie Kat. "Do you ever get on each other's nerves, packed into that small space after having houses of your own?"

"All the time. That's the fun of it. When we lived separately, we had to put on clothes to go find someone to argue with. Now we can argue in our nighties. It's terrific."

He laughed, but her phrase stuck with him. *Someone to argue with*. She'd said it with affection, and he'd heard those women sparring with each other. It was the kind of teasing that grew out of love and years of friendship.

His mom and dad used to do it all the time. Adam and Tracy were falling into that pattern. Luis and Jordan, too. Mila and Cole were still acting like newlyweds, but he could see them settling into that kind of relationship soon.

He envied them. He'd enjoyed trading barbs with his siblings, especially when he and his brothers shared the bunkhouse, but now that they all lived separately, it wasn't the same.

Was there something about shared living quarters that created the dynamic? If so, and he stayed on his current trajectory, he wouldn't—

"Looks like I'll need to start this conversation."

He blinked. "Sorry. Something you said got me to thinking."

"About?"

"The benefits of living with someone."

"If you want to invite Zinnia to live with you, we're all for it."

"I won't be doing that." Yikes. Never occurred to him.

"Why not? You might need to wait a few days because it might be too soon to move that foal, but—"

"Grandma, none of that's happening. Zinnia and I have decided to back off."

"Back off?" Her blue eyes widened and she put down her coffee. "Are you nuts?"

"Probably. But I'm not ready to be that little guy's father."

"Tell that to someone who didn't see how you patiently waited while he opened all your presents. You should have seen your face. In fact, I might have a picture on my phone. I left it in the house. Stay here and I'll get it."

"It doesn't matter how I looked. I'm not—"

"Stay put, please. I'll be right back."

He sighed. Once again, his impulse to be nice to Tex was biting him in the butt. So what if he looked fatherly in a picture? That didn't make him a father, for God's sake.

She reappeared, definitely on a mission. Usually she looked angelic with her white curls and pink cheeks. But when she got a bee in her bonnet, as Auntie Kat liked to say, she was a force of nature.

"Look at this." She held out the phone. "There's more than one. Scroll through them all. And then tell me you're not ready to be his father."

"Yes, ma'am." They'd all learned at an early age that when Grandma Doris took that tone, they'd better do as she said or there'd be hell to pay. They'd suddenly find themselves assigned to the nastiest chores on the ranch.

She'd taken a ton of pictures. He flipped through them and handed back the phone.

She refused to take it. "Go through them again, please. Slowly."

"Yes, ma'am." Bracing himself, he focused on each frame. He couldn't argue with her conclusion. Any stranger who saw these shots would assume he was the dad of this serious little boy.

She'd even taken a video of Tex watching him pull off every blessed strip of tape the kid had stuck on the wrapping for Rance's book. The video continued, recording his pleasure at seeing the book's cover and Tex jumping up and down with joy. Pure joy.

His throat tightened.

"You love him."

He nodded.

"Do you love her?"

"I don't know."

"Yes, you do. You just haven't admitted it to yourself."

He glanced up. "You can't fall in love that fast."

"Oh, no? Your father did with Raquel."

"And look what happened!"

"What do you mean? It all worked out. They had a wonderful—"

"And then he died!"

"Is that what you're afraid of? Is that why you're *backing off*?" She made air quotes.

"No. I mean, yes, but it's taking on the responsibility of a family that makes me nervous. I'm not ready for that."

"Hm. Care to elaborate?"

"The way I see it, you do your best, and your family comes to depend on you, and then you die and pull the rug out from under them. I don't want to put Zinnia and Tex through that. Or anyone."

"You're planning to stay single?"

"For now. Maybe someday I'll change my mind, but at this stage, it's not for me."

She didn't say anything for a while, just gazed out toward the pasture where the horses grazed, tails flicking away random flies as they savored new grass and warm sunlight.

Finally she turned and picked up a sticky bun. "I'm having one of these. Kat can just suck it."

"What?"

"She's on us a lot about our diet and she's right. We'll all live longer and be healthier because of her, but sometimes you just need a sticky bun."

"True." He followed her lead. "If everyone swore off sticky buns, Greta would go out of business." Maybe their conversation about Zinnia and Tex was over.

"Exactly. If you don't pig out, you'll be okay. I also need to ditch this coffee and get a refill."

"Let me." He held out his hand but she waved it away.

"Thanks. I've got it." Putting the half-eaten bun on a napkin, she stood, walked over to the railing and poured the cold coffee in the flowerbed where iris had just started poking out. "Looking good."

"I put mulch on them last fall."

"Noticed that. You take excellent care of this place." She came back with her mug.

"Because I love living here." He reached for her mug and poured her a fresh cup from the carafe.

"Alone?"

"You did." He handed over the coffee and she settled back in the rocker.

"I was technically alone, but you kids were always over here, even spending the night sometimes. I didn't feel alone." Picking up the rest of her sticky bun, she took a generous bite.

"Neither do I." He wasn't sure that was true. Waking up to find Zinnia gone had been a lonely experience. Coming home to an empty house after the party last night hadn't felt great, either.

"You never got to meet your Grandpa Bridger."

"Which makes my point. That had to be tough on you and Dad, just like it was for everyone when Dad passed."

"It was, but I wouldn't change anything. Well, maybe I'd be more forceful about changing Joe's diet. Kat and I both tried, then tried again with Spence. Those two were so alike."

"And I'm my father's son. So's Adam, for that matter."

"Do you think he made a mistake marrying Tracy?"

"I have to wonder if he's thought about his odds."

"I don't know if he has or not, but I'd say his odds are excellent. He'll live a long, happy life."

"Why? He works too hard and takes on too many obligations just like Dad. Heart problems run in the family, at least for the men."

"What you said is true, but it doesn't have to be a death sentence. According to his doctor, Joe could have beat the odds by doing two things — eat better and ditch the belief that the fate of the world rests on his shoulders."

"That sounds familiar. Mom used to say that to Dad. Something like *the world won't end if you don't do such and such.*"

"But he didn't believe it. Neither did Joe. They bought into the myth they had to do everything, fix everything. Not being able to save your mother was unacceptable to Spence and it was slowly killing him. I could see it."

"Just a couple days ago Graham told me why he insisted on calling me Montgomery."

"Spence never told you?"

"Nope."

"Shame on him. Wish I'd known that. Anyway, he took his cue from his dad and lived his life the same way Joe did. You might see Adam doing the same, but he isn't."

"Looks like it to me. He's got all his responsibilities here and now he's the mayor, just like Dad was."

"It's partly Tracy's influence that keeps him from over-estimating his importance in the grand scheme of things."

"Interesting way of putting it. You think Dad did that? Thought he was more important than he was?"

"I know it sounds critical, but basically, yes. Joe did the same. But Tracy grew up with a father who doesn't buy into the all-powerful savior role. Whenever Adam starts sounding like he's Atlas holding up the town, she calls him on it. I've seen her do it."

"Huh. I might have heard her do that, too. But does he listen? Dad never did."

"He does listen. He loved your dad. We all did, but Adam doesn't want to end up dying in his fifties under the weight of that kind of thinking."

"I guess I'm not as much like Dad as I thought. I don't consider myself some all-powerful savior."

"But you think you have to be."

"No, I don't. It's just the odds I don't like."

"What if you can change the odds? What if Zinnia, who's a strong person who doesn't require a savior, could help you change those odds?"

"Maybe she could. I get your point about Tracy being a good influence on Adam. I have noticed he doesn't eat like Dad and if Zinnia knew about the heart thing, she'd be on it."

"Because she's in love with you just like you're in love with her."

"I'm not sure about that." But it created warmth in his chest to hear her say it, even if Zinnia never told him.

"Then I guess you haven't been paying attention. Everyone else can see it."

"You notice Adam and Tracy haven't had kids yet."

"I've noticed. They're busy with the town council."

"Or maybe Adam's nervous about having kids. Maybe the heart thing still bothers him the way it bothers me."

"I doubt it, but that might be an interesting conversation for you to have with him."

"At least he'd start with a baby. I don't know anything about raising a five-year-old. I'd screw that up, for sure."

"So could Zinnia. Parents make mistakes all the time."

"Yeah, but I'm this person coming in partway through the story, learning on the fly. I'm bound to let that kid down, and he—"

"He'd be fine. Listen, Monty. Having a dad like yours can make it look like husbands and fathers are required to be superhuman. Some even get away with it. Joe couldn't. Spence couldn't."

"I see what you're saying."

"Do you? Because I think you're still caught up in the idea that you have to be a perfect father for Tex, just like you have to be a perfect vet, sacrificing sleep to stay overnight with a sick horse or a pregnant mare. And if you can't, then you hook up those cameras of yours and monitor your phone constantly."

"It's called being good at my job."

"I've heard Graham calls you Supervet."

"It's a joke, Grandma."

She speared him with a blue-eyed gaze that saw way too much. "Is it?"

28

Thank goodness Tex had babbled nonstop on the way home from the party. If he'd fallen asleep in his car seat as usual, Uncle Graham would have had questions Zinnia wouldn't have wanted to answer.

She'd had quite a challenge getting Tex to calm down long enough to tuck him in bed. By the time he'd finally gone to sleep, her uncle had given up and hit the sack himself.

Much as she'd wanted to stay awake until Mari got home, she hadn't been able to keep her eyes open. Some insomniac she was. Maybe the Monty effect was still in force because she'd slept soundly until the rising sun ushered in a bizarro day.

Mari kept trying to get info on the party and the only person who gave her an unfiltered response was Tex. He had a new audience and was thrilled to chatter away about his experiences.

Meanwhile Uncle Graham kept giving her looks as if he was dying to quiz her. She pretended not to notice. Then Mari started with the looks, but with Tex constantly around, she sure wasn't going to get into it.

Finding a private moment with her sister when either Tex or her uncle weren't in the room proved impossible. She'd hoped Tex would take a nap to make up for his late night, but no dice.

Then finally, soon after dinner, he ran out of juice. She had no trouble getting him to bed and he was asleep before she left his room.

As she walked down the hall, Mari and Uncle Graham's voices in the kitchen were pitched low, as if they wanted to make sure Tex couldn't hear. She sucked in a breath and went to join them.

They both glanced up, Uncle Graham giving her a benevolent smile and Mari's gaze full of questions she wouldn't ask in front of their uncle.

"No worries. He went out like a light."

"That's good." Uncle Graham let out a sigh of relief. "I've been telling Mari it looks like you and Monty have something going on, but I don't want to jump to too many conclusions."

"I appreciate that." She took a seat at the old oak table next to Mari. "Monty and I do have affection for each other. I guess that was obvious to everyone at the party."

Her uncle grinned. "Sure was. I was tickled to see it, too. I won't say I told you so, but... I told you so."

"The thing is, we've agreed to back off."

Mari ducked her head to hide a smile. She'd likely assumed that was the cover story.

But her uncle looked confused. "Why?"

"Basically, because of Tex."

"Tex? He thinks Monty hung the moon!"

"I know, but—"

"And Monty seems to really care about Tex. I have pictures of them doing the present thing and it was remarkable how they acted like father and son. Raquel was impressed, too."

"Monty does love him."

"See? I knew it. And it's obvious you and Monty clicked, so what's the problem?"

"Monty's not ready to take on that kind of responsibility."

"He said that? I can't imagine him saying that."

"But he did, and I admire him for being honest. I wish my ex had been that honest with me."

"He just needs more time to think about it, to get used to the idea."

"That's exactly what I told myself about my ex, but it never happened. I'm not making that mistake twice."

"I guarantee Monty is nothing like your ex. I suppose it's only natural he's a little nervous about becoming an instant father, but all you have to do is look at my pictures and you'll see he'd be great at it."

"I watched that whole thing, too, and it made me want to cry. Tex would love to have someone like Monty in his life, but if a man says he's not up to the job, I'll by God believe him."

His expression softened. "My apologies, sweetheart. Pay me no mind. Guess I was too invested in the fairytale ending."

"You weren't the only one. I don't regret going to the party. Tex had a blast. But now Monty's whole family thinks…." She sighed. "I guess they'll get over it."

"I have a question." Mari was looking at her, and the smile was gone. Had she figured out the affair was over, too? Probably. "If you and Monty aren't pursuing this romance, will the Bridgers still want to socialize with us?"

"I'll answer that." Uncle Graham sat up straighter. "That family is true blue. They welcomed Zin and Tex the way I knew they would, and they won't suddenly go cold because of this. That's not how they're made."

"I'll second that." Zinnia gazed at her sister. "Sure, they'll be disappointed about Monty and me, but they're not petty. They won't judge. I can't wait for you to meet everyone. You'll love them."

"I can't wait, either. I'm glad we'll still be welcome. They sound like fun."

"They are." Would she have some awkward moments? Yes, but that was on her. They'd be as lovely as ever.

The discussion then turned to Monty the Colt. Mari had suggested that label the day before, and even Tex had thought it sounded cool.

Zinnia had already shortened it, calling him MTC. Yes, it sounded like she was saying Empty Sea, which was ridiculous, but she was desperate to eliminate the name Monty from her life. Was she insane to go over there tonight?

As if Fate had decided to throw a monkey wrench—haha—into their rendezvous plan, Uncle Graham chose to stay up later than usual. She considered ducking into her bedroom and texting Monty to cancel. Couldn't seem to do it.

The minute Uncle Graham bid them goodnight and walked into his room, Mari grabbed her by the arm and motioned toward the front porch. She followed her sister out and took one of the Adirondack chairs.

"Are you really calling it quits? Even the sex?"

"Yes."

"Aw, Zin."

"Last night he asked for one more night, so I'm supposed to go over there, but I'm wondering if that's smart."

"Because someone might see you?"

"No. It's totally chill over there late at night. But why dig myself in deeper? I'll just miss him that much more."

"Are you in love with him?"

"Afraid so. Which is stupid. You can't be in love with someone you just met."

"Sure you can. Happens all the time. Sometimes it lasts and sometimes it doesn't."

"Well, this episode is doomed, so I might just be torturing myself unnecessarily if I go over there."

"Your call."

"I know."

"Uncle Graham showed me those pictures while you were putting Tex to bed."

"I figured he might have."

"He's right. Monty looks like a doting father."

"He looked exactly like that, which is what makes this so effing hard. Maybe he would come around, but I've been burned before."

"Maybe I shouldn't have talked you into having sex with him. I'm starting to feel bad about that."

"Well, don't. Celibacy isn't all it's cracked up to be."

Mari laughed. "Good one. So are you okay with spending time at that ranch? I know what you said, but if it's problematic for you, then…."

"I like them so much that I'll power through any awkward moments. Raquel's wonderful. They all are. Oh, and remember Uncle Graham telling us about the Jordan Sterling training center over there?"

"I do. Sounded like a big deal."

"I didn't get a look at it, but I'm sure it's awesome. And Jordan offered to help train Tex and MTC."

"Won't that be expensive?"

"She's giving me a discount."

"Are you sure the Monty situation won't affect that?"

"It won't. We need to remember that Spence Bridger was best friends with our uncle. They used to hang out all the time. He's the reason everyone's so friendly to us. They love him."

"Then lucky us, huh?"

"We are. There's one other thing I haven't told you, but you have to promise not to let on you know."

"Ooo, a secret. I love secrets."

"I'm aware. So, have you noticed how many times our uncle mentions Raquel?"

"Now that you say that, he does talk about her a lot." Her breath caught. "Are you saying—"

"He's got a huge crush."

"*No.*" She giggled. "Now I really have to meet this woman. Is she good enough for him?"

"I'm guessing he doesn't think he's good enough for her. Spence Bridger would be a tough act to follow."

"Maybe, but Uncle Graham's no slouch, either. I thought he was through with women, though."

"So did I. Then I saw him light up on Thursday morning when we were there for the shoeing appointment. Yesterday whenever I went looking for him, he was with Raquel."

"Does she know?"

"I'm not sure. I don't know her well enough to be able to say. She looked happy, though, and he makes her laugh."

"That's so cool. After putting up with Aunt Adele, he deserves another shot." She exhaled. "And so do you. I'm sorry this isn't it."

"Me, too."

"Gonna go over there?"

"God help me, I am."

29

Dressed in his sweats, Monty paced from the living room to the bedroom as he waited for Zinnia. She'd be here. If she'd decided to bail she would have let him know by now.

On his trips into the bedroom he often paused to look at the family pictures on the desk. His dad was in all of them.

He hadn't made the opportunity to talk with Adam today like his grandma had suggested. He had no excuse. Sunday would have been a perfect time to snag Adam for a private chat.

But he'd procrastinated until it was too late. He'd told himself he needed time to process this morning's conversation. His grandma could be right about him. For one thing, he had a tendency to overwork.

He also liked Graham calling him Supervet. He always passed off the comment as a joke, but the farrier wasn't joking. He admired that level of dedication to a career. Praise from him was special because it meant he measured up to the standards his dad had set.

His dad had been good at everything. He had a vivid picture of one Christmas when the living room had been a chaotic scene with all eight kids racing around through wads of wrapping paper, new toys and new clothes. His mom had been trying to restore order without much success.

His dad had let out a piercing whistle, the kind he made through his teeth. Monty and his siblings had frozen in place, sure they were in big trouble.

Then his dad had bellowed *Get dressed! Touch football in the snow! You've got seven minutes!*

Why he'd chosen seven minutes instead of five or ten was a mystery. Maybe just to focus their attention because it was an unusual time interval.

His mom had given his dad an adoring look and said *You were born to be a father.*

Born to be a father. Sure had seemed that way. He'd happily helped produce three, married a woman who had three more, and had been thrilled to add another two.

He'd taught them everything he knew about horses. Then he'd taught them everything he knew about construction. He'd been the town's most popular mayor, although Adam might overtake him on that score. He'd been famous for saying any disagreement could be settled over a beer.

Hey, was that where he'd gone wrong with his grandma? Should he have served her a beer at four in the afternoon instead of coffee at ten in the morning? He snorted.

He didn't need that strategy for Zinnia because he had no disagreements with her. They were in complete agreement that they should pour gallons of water on this fire they'd started.

He wanted to blame her for lighting the match, but he could have blown it out. Yeah, right. Never would have happened.

Sadly, if his grandma was right about him, he was rejecting fatherhood because he couldn't live up to the example his father had set. Who could? Was that why Adam hadn't—

Zinnia's truck pulled up outside, the engine's rumble muffled by the closed window. He'd shut them an hour ago so he wouldn't forget.

Heart pumping, he hurried out to the porch. She'd parked to the left of his house. Technically it wasn't a parking space, but she'd managed to squeeze her truck in so it was somewhat hidden by trees.

Now that his whole family knew they were involved, she didn't have to do that. After yesterday nobody would be surprised to see it there. And she'd never park there again. His gut clenched.

She hopped out of the driver's side and closed the door gently. No little cross-body bag tonight. No keys in her hand. She'd likely figured out that on Bridger property she could leave them in the truck.

He headed down to meet her, skin tingling with anticipation. He'd gone barefoot as a kid, but hardly ever as an adult. The smooth wood of the steps and the tickle of grass caressed the bottoms of his feet.

Wind sighing through the trees mingled with the rustle and pop of her sandals, the swish of her filmy nightgown, the sound of her quick, shallow breaths.

His nostrils flared, taking in the brisk fragrance of pines and crushed grass, the sweetness of wild roses and Zinnia's citrus scent. Moonlight touched her pale hair and skin, giving her an other-worldly glow.

They came together with an ease that made his heart weep. He had the insane urge to strip off his sweats and make love to her on the soft grass.

Nestling against him, winding her arms around his neck, she lifted her face to his. "I've missed you."

His throat tightened. "I've missed you, too." He sounded gruff, almost angry. And maybe he was. At himself. He wasn't the man she needed.

But he kissed her anyway. She'd granted him one more night and he'd make it a memorable one even if it killed him.

She kissed him back, and at first he tasted longing and regret. But soon enough, the mood shifted and the white-hot passion neither of them could snuff out roared to life.

Pushing her nightgown up over her hips, he spread both hands over her tush and tugged her close. Gasping, he lifted his mouth from hers. "If I had a blanket I'd take you right here."

She took a gulp of air. "If you had a blanket I'd let you."

"No blanket."

"Then let's get inside." Breaking away from him, she grabbed his hand and pulled him toward the steps.

He stumbled after her. He hadn't meant to leave the door open when he'd hurried outside.

Showed how distracted he'd been. With luck some critter hadn't wandered in while he'd been totally occupied kissing Zinnia.

Nothing went scurrying away as they came in, so he'd assume all was well. "Door." He pulled her to a halt so he could close it.

"See you in there." She let go of his hand, kicked off her flip-flops and ran down the hall.

Running wasn't an option in his current state. By the time he joined her in the bedroom, she'd tossed off her nightgown and opened the condom drawer.

"Catch." She tossed him one.

By some miracle he plucked it out of the air before it hit the floor, saving himself the humiliation of hunting for it. Holding the packet in his teeth, he shucked his sweats and ripped open the foil.

"I almost didn't come."

He glanced up. "But you will, now."

She smiled. "Haha. Looking forward to it."

"So am I." He finished rolling on the condom and took stock of the situation. Thank God he'd asked for one more night, one more chance to see her like this.

She lay stretched out in all her golden-girl glory, looking exactly the way he'd pictured her when he'd put on clean sheets this afternoon. He'd pulled the top sheet and blanket down, leaving them folded at the bottom. With Zinnia in his bed, he didn't need covers.

She beckoned to him. "C'mere, you. Make the world go away."

"Can I do that?" He climbed in, holding her gaze as he moved between her thighs.

"Sure can. You're magic."

He kept eye contact, loving how the emerald green darkened, her cheeks flushed and her lips parted. "So are you." Her heat called to him, but he held off. This moment, anticipating the joy of sinking into her, was precious. "When I'm loving you, the world disappears."

"I should hope so." She rested her palms on his chest and fooled with his nipples, making his cock twitch. "I'd hate to think that while I'm blissed out, you're worrying about a sick horse."

He grimaced. "I've been known to."

"Me, too." She cupped his face in both hands, making him glad he'd shaved. "Not a sick horse, but other stuff. When I'm with you, I forget everything and everybody." She smiled. "Or I will, once you get busy."

His cock throbbed. "Yes, ma'am." He rocked forward, closing his eyes and dragging in air as pleasure rolled through him. He almost missed her murmured *I gots you.*

Slowly he opened his eyes and gazed into hers. His brain stalled. She loved him.

And he loved her with a fierceness that burned in his chest. The words almost came out of his mouth. He swallowed them. Proclaiming it wouldn't do either of them any favors.

"I gots you, too." Leaning down, he kissed her rosy lips as he began to thrust. She joined in, hooking her legs around his, linking them together, synchronizing their movements.

His energy level spiked as he immersed himself in her heat and breathless cries. When he was loving Zinnia, he knew what to do. It came so easily, as if he'd been born knowing.

She was panting now. *There*. The first squeeze of her climax teased his cock and he stroked faster, the pressure in his groin increasing. If he tamed his response, he could make her come again. Didn't feel right. He needed... no *they* needed to ride the rapids together, plunge over the edge together.

Her body quivered and her skin glowed in the lamplight. This would be good. Really good. She called his name, grabbed onto him and arched upward. One more vigorous push.... Ahhh. She came apart, loudly, joyfully.

Her orgasm triggered his, ripping a shout of triumph from his ecstatic, shaking body. She held him close, absorbing his tremors as he absorbed hers.

The room filled with the sound of their gasps and soft moans. And then it was quiet.

He stayed where he was, propped on his forearms, his head bowed. They were perfect together. Some men never experienced lovemaking they would treasure the rest of their lives.

He just had. It would have to be enough.

30

Zinnia lay still, afraid to move and break the spell. Friday night she'd had sex with Monty. Tonight, she'd made love with him. Big difference. For the first time in her life, she got it.

This cowboy she'd just met had made love with his whole body and soul. He'd cherished her. He'd delighted in her lusty spirit. She'd been seen.

He was also madly in love with her. And she with him. But love wasn't enough, not when a five-year-old was in the mix.

Kissing her gently on her forehead, he looked into her eyes, his gaze warm. "You're wonderful."

Even if he didn't say the words, they hovered in the air, a bittersweet reminder of what could have been. "You, too."

"Gotta take care of—"

"I know." She unwound her legs from his. "You're free to go." Her breath hitched. Was this the end? Kenny Rogers' voice echoed in her ears. Was the dealing done?

Maybe. She wasn't accomplished in the art of saying goodbye.

Was this the right time, after lovemaking so amazing it had almost been a spiritual experience? Should they end on a high note rather than chance having things go downhill from here?

Trouble was, she wanted to find out if his grandma had paid him a visit and if so, how the family had reacted to the news that they weren't pursuing this relationship. Once she left his cottage, her chances of having a private conversation with him would be limited.

Propping a pillow against the headboard, she sat up. Did she want to make love again? Yes, of course. Always. But....

They ran the risk of letting sadness creep in the next time. They'd successfully blocked it so far, but how long before it overshadowed the pleasure?

"When I left you were smiling. Now you're frowning. What's up?"

She watched him walk over to the bed and her heart stuttered. So beautiful. So out of reach. If he'd had some big announcement about a change of heart he would have made it before they climbed into this bed.

Or not. He might broach it now. Had she been secretly hoping she'd arrive and discover he'd had an epiphany? Sure looked like it.

If he had changed his mind, she'd still be wary of diving into a relationship that was in full view of his family. And Tex. But she'd at least consider it.

She sucked in a breath. "I was just wondering if you'd talked with your grandmother?"

"Yes. This morning." He laid a pillow against the headboard, got in and leaned against it.

Then he reached for her hand and gazed at her. "Are you worried about how my family's reacting to us nipping this in the bud?"

He hadn't changed his mind. The bubble of hope she'd allowed to grow burst, leaving icky, sticky emotions behind. "I guess. Uncle Graham says it won't change the way they think about me and Tex. And Mari, when she eventually meets them."

"It won't." He squeezed her hand. "If anything, they're probably wondering what's wrong with me, backing away from a beautiful woman and an adorable kid."

"You haven't talked to anyone else?"

"Not yet. It may be coming. Grandma and I sat out on the porch. She wanted us to be seen since she was the official representative from the family. They'll go to her first."

"You think they'll be upset with you?"

"I doubt it. Disappointed, maybe."

He didn't deserve that. "Look, I'm the one who started this. I'll bet you didn't share that with your grandmother."

"No, and I won't. Not with her, or anyone. You were ready to leave, but I knocked myself out convincing you to stay. Even talked you into showing up tonight. We created this situation together."

"Okay, but they need to give you credit for having valid concerns about how our situation would affect Tex. That's realistic on your part. Wise, even."

He snorted and glanced away. "My grandma thinks I'm more scared than wise."

"It's perfectly normal to be scared. All you wanted was fun and games. Then suddenly you're expected to make life-changing decisions."

A muscle in his jaw tightened. "Thank you for that, but—"

"Seriously, I get why you don't want to suddenly take on a mom and her kid."

Dragging in a breath, he turned to face her. "My grandma's right. I'm terrified. I'm not a good bet, Zinnia. I could really screw things up for you."

"If you say so." She could argue the point, but she'd be going against her own advice. Never talk a man into marriage or fatherhood. Been there, done that, bought the T-shirt.

His attention shifted to the desk with the family pictures on it. "There are so many ways I could get it wrong. Spend too much time on my career and mess up as a father. Spend too much time being a father and sabotage my career. Make sure I excel at both and ignore you. Or, and this is the scenario that freaks me out the most — I could push myself to be great at everything and end up like my father, dying in my fifties."

"*What*?"

"My dad was an overachiever. They used to call them Type-A personalities and they're usually men. They're determined to be good at everything they take on. That tendency's particularly dangerous if heart problems run in the family."

"You have a heart problem?" She pressed a hand to her chest. "Why didn't you say—"

"I don't have one now, but I'm genetically predisposed, something I tend to ignore. At least I think I ignore it, but I may be kidding myself about that."

"What about Adam? Is he worried about this?"

"I don't know. Haven't discussed it with him. My grandma suggested I do that. For all I know he's decided against having kids to make it easier on Tracy if he follows the pattern."

"Is there a pattern?"

He nodded. "My grandfather and great-grandfather also died of heart attacks in their mid-fifties." He glanced at her. "Until now, I've shoved all of this to the back of my mind."

She struggled to absorb what he was saying. "Am I the one that stirred it all up, then?"

"You did." He let go of her hand and cupped her face. "And I don't regret anything. Well, that's not true. I regret I can't be the man you and Tex need."

"But what if you could beat the odds?" The minute the words popped out, she wanted them back. She was *not* going down that road.

"What if I can't?"

And there it was. He'd convinced himself the stakes were too high. The game was over.

31

The glow faded from Zinnia's eyes. "I'd better go."

Monty opened his mouth to protest. Closed it again. "Okay."

When she left the bed, so did he. Putting on his sweats while she put on her nightgown, he walked her to the door and opened it for her. "Take care."

"You, too." She didn't look at him. Likely she was crying.

Damned if he wasn't fighting tears, too. He closed the door and stood there with his hand on the knob, his body cold and stiff, as if he was incased in a block of ice.

She didn't start the truck right away. For one crazy second he thought she might come back. Then the engine sputtered to life.

He didn't move until the sound of the truck was completely gone. Going back to the bed wasn't an option, so he dropped down into the closest easy chair. He was still there when the birds woke him in the morning.

Over the next few days, he kidded himself that he looked and acted completely normal. Whenever a member of his family approached him, he met them with a big smile and talked about the weather.

So far nobody had tried to break through the invisible fence he'd erected, and he was grateful. He needed time, and they were honoring that.

He briefly considered talking things out with Adam. In the end he couldn't see the point in baring his soul when it was still bleeding.

He'd convinced Zinnia to give up on him for her own good. He'd count that as a victory and move on. Somehow.

Staying busy kept her out of his head during the day, but the nights were hell. He'd forced himself to sleep in his bed because the chair was doing a number on his spine.

Although his back pain went away, Zinnia filled his dreams and he'd wake up with a hole in his heart he could drive a truck through. But he'd saved her, saved her and Tex. That was all that mattered.

At the two-week mark, not that he was counting, he woke in the pre-dawn hours with a start. Something wasn't right. Lying in the dark, he listened for what might have broken into his sleep.

Nothing out of the ordinary. Crickets chirped and an owl hooted in the distance. Then his phone rang. *Zinnia.*

His heart pounding, he answered. "Are you okay?"

"Tex is gone." She was breathing fast. "I think he went to find you."

"Dear God. I'm on my way." Leaping out of bed, he laid the phone down as he threw on his clothes. "How long has he—"

"Not sure. He took brownies." She gulped. "We've been driving the road, calling out, but he—I th-think he's h-hiding." Her voice shook.

He clamped down on his own terror so he wouldn't add to hers. "Why?"

"Brownies. He wants to s-surprise you with brownies."

"Hang tight. We'll find him." He started to disconnect, then paused. "I love you."

"I love you, too. Hurry."

"I will." He called Adam. "Tex apparently decided to set out alone to bring me brownies. I'm going over there to—"

"No, we're going. I'll drive. You get Zinnia back on the line so we can coordinate our efforts."

"Great idea. I'll be right over." On his way out the door he grabbed a first-aid kit from the bathroom, a blanket from the hall closet and his handheld spotlight. No telling what that little guy had gotten himself into.

But he'd be fine. Had to be fine. He wouldn't let himself imagine any other outcome.

As he ran toward Adam and Tracy's cabin, his mom and Greta came out of the main house pulling on sweatshirts.

"We're going," Greta said.

"How did—"

"Adam sent a group text while he was talking to you."

"I'll be damned."

"We're taking our truck, too," Luis called out as he and Jordan emerged from their casita. "Rio and Zay are with us. Mila's bringing everybody else in the van. The more people we have, the better our chances of finding him."

"Can't argue with that!" His voice sounded a little froggy. His throat had a boulder-sized lump in it. The Bridger Bunch had gathered.

He took the front passenger seat while Tracy, Greta and his mom sat in back. Once they were on their way, he called Zinnia.

She answered immediately. "Still no luck." Her voice was tight with fear. "I just know he's out there determined to get to you before we get to him. He's such a st-stubborn little c-cuss."

His chest ached. She was trying so hard not to lose it. "Help is on the way. I'm in Adam's truck with my mom, Tracy and Greta. Luis is behind us with Jordan, Zay and Rio. Mila's bringing everyone else in the van."

There was a choked sound on the other end. "They all..." Then came a loud sniff and a deep exhale. "Tell them...tell them...thank you."

"You're welcome!" Greta, Tracy and his mom sang out in unison.

"They figured more people looking would be—"

"It's brilliant." She took a shaky breath. "He loves all of you. He'll come out for sure. Should we stop calling to him?"

"Maybe." He glanced at Adam, who nodded. "Yeah, why not try that. We just went through the front gate. I doubt he got this far."

"I'm sure not. But he might have made it to the main road." She sounded slightly calmer.

He had his family to thank for that. "At least there's no traffic at this time." He chose not to give voice to what else could be out there.

"Right. Let me talk to Mari and my uncle for a sec." After some murmuring in the background, she came back. "We've decided to drive back home and let your caravan take it from here."

"Okay. But stay on the phone."

"Oh, you know it. You're my lifeline right now."

Her words punched him right in the gut. He must have let out a little gasp because Adam gave him a look.

Then his big brother pulled out his phone and called Luis. "I'll set the pace, amigo. We'll roll down our windows and take turns calling for Tex. Identify yourselves when you call out so he knows it's us. Pass that word to Mila. If anybody hears or sees anything, give a holler."

What followed reminded Monty of a weird nighttime version of the Fourth of July parade. Except it was being staged for one small spectator. At Adam's suggestion, he took more turns than anyone.

If the circumstances weren't so scary, he'd get a kick out of the various bribes his family came up with. Auntie Ezzie offered to teach him new cha-cha steps. Rio said he could sit in his lap and steer the Gator.

Greta promised sticky buns and his mom dangled a trip to the attic where the toys were stored. Cole said he could flip the switch to start the Beaver Bunch show. Claudie invited him to look over her supply of colored tape. No response. The woods on either side of the road were dark and still.

About fifty yards from the turnoff to Graham's road, Adam pointed to him and he launched into his spiel.

"Hey, sport, it's Mister Monty!" He worked hard to make his voice sound jovial. Wasn't easy when the spotlight he swept over the bushes and trees sometimes reflected a pair of glowing eyes.

Instead of going for a bribe, he zeroed in on what Zinnia thought Tex wanted out of this escapade. "I hear you have a surprise for me. Can't wait to see what it is!"

Something rustled in the bushes. Could be a critter.

He murmured to Adam, who stopped the truck. Instead of pointing the spotlight right at the bush, he directed it toward the shoulder of the road. Didn't want to blind the kid if it was him.

Tex walked out holding Smokey under his arm and a well-taped package in his other hand. Looked like he'd chosen cowboy-themed paper to wrap the brownies. His hat was on crooked and he was smudged with dirt everywhere — face, arms, T-shirt and jeans.

Giddy with relief, he reached for the door hand. Joy surged through him, pushing away the fog that had clouded his thinking for days.

How had he missed the obvious? His dad had been a solo act. Adam was not. More important, *he* was not. Instead of dashing off on his own, he'd called Adam. Adam had called the Bridger Bunch. None of them had to do it all.

So why was he fighting his love for Zinnia and Tex when he had a whole team behind him? Only an idiot would do that, and his dad hadn't raised an idiot.

He stepped out of the truck. "Zinnia, I've got him. I've got Tex."

32

Uncle Graham's house wasn't big enough for the Bridger Bunch, but the Dazzling Damsels insisted it would work. Zinnia coaxed Mari into turning the kitchen over to them.

At least they had plenty of food in the house. She and Mari had shopped the day before. They'd have to shop again tomorrow, but who cared? Tex was safe and sound.

Those ladies unearthed a stash of paper plates and plastic utensils that Uncle Graham had forgotten he had. Breakfast was served buffet style and eaten in various venues, including out in the barn.

Everyone took turns visiting Speckles and her foal. Tex stuck to Monty as if they were taped together. She and Monty would have to talk about this episode, but she was exhausted and wanted to savor this joyous moment a little longer.

She and Mari ended up sitting on the porch steps with Raquel and Uncle Graham and balancing their plates on their laps.

"I can't believe I've never been over here, Graham." Raquel glanced at him. "How is that possible?"

"To be honest, Adele didn't like to entertain. But now that she's gone, I'd love to have you over for dinner some night."

"That sounds like fun."

Mari nudged Zinnia with her foot. "Uncle Graham's a good cook, Raquel. I do most of it because that's only fair considering how good he's been to us, but every so often he'll insist on making one of his specialties. We always look forward to those nights."

"I didn't know that about you, Graham."

"Mari's laying it on a little thick, so don't go expecting a five-star restaurant, but I do enjoy messing around in the kitchen."

Zinnia didn't dare look at Mari since they had to be putting the same spin on that comment. Engineering a night alone for these two would take fancy footwork, though. Maybe she and Tex could visit Jordan and Luis on a night Mari was working.

"Hey, Zinnia, could I talk to you for a minute?"

She glanced up. There stood Monty, his morning beard shadowing his chiseled jawline, a light in his blue eyes that made her catch her breath. Tex was nowhere around.

Don't get your hopes up, girlfriend. "Um, sure." She looked at her empty plate. "Let me just get rid of—"

"I'll take it." Mari whisked it out of her hands.

"Thanks, Mar." As she started to get up, Monty held out his hand.

She took it. His firm grip set off a predictable reaction. The last time she'd held his hand they'd been naked. But that was over. Wasn't it?

The fact that he continued holding her hand as they walked away from the porch was confusing as hell. "Where's Tex?"

"He's showing Rio how to sit on the bucket and make friends with his foal."

"I'll bet that's fun to watch."

"Could be, I suppose." He kept walking, passing the lineup of vehicles until they reached the van at the end. Then he glanced over his shoulder. "Good. Nobody's paying attention. Let's skedaddle around to the other side of the van."

"Monty. I thought we had an agreement." But she went, anyway. If he was about to ask if she'd resume their affair, could she resist the temptation?

"We did." Taking off his hat and setting it on the roof of the van, he pulled her close. "If you want to keep things the way they've been the past two weeks…." He paused. "I'll find a way to live with it."

"You want to continue our affair?"

"No. I want to marry you."

Her world shifted under the weight of those words. But they made no sense. "No, you don't."

"Yes, I do. The shock of Tex going missing might have been enough to show me what an idiot I've been. I went crazy thinking something might happen to that little guy. But then my family showed up to help find him and that was the clincher."

"What does your family searching for Tex have to do with us?"

"It convinced me Adam's nothing like my dad. My brother doesn't handle everything himself. He calls for help from the rest of us. Turns out, so do I. And by the way, Tracy's pretty sure she's pregnant but she hasn't confirmed it so keep that to yourself."

"I will, but—"

"I talked to Adam just now. He has no qualms about having kids and he plans to live a long time." He sucked in a breath. "So do I. I'd love to spend that long life with you and Tex. If you'll have me."

"You're giving me whiplash." He was also melting the resistance she'd worked so hard to create. "You were so sure you'd get it wrong and screw up our lives. You made a believer of me."

"Oh, I'll get things wrong. But I won't screw up your lives because my family is there to help me correct course. They'll remind me if I start sounding like a one-man show who can do it all."

"And you'll listen?"

"You bet I will if the reward is you and Tex." His brow furrowed. "But I can't do anything about the short timeline. Nobody would blame you for saying you don't know me well enough to make that decision. The thing is, Tex has already made his. He's stuck on me and it looks like we can't unstick him."

Tape. He was referencing her son's fascination with tape. A loving father would do that. He was getting to her, burrowing under her defenses, making her a believer.

"One other thing. Instant attraction also runs in my family. My dad met our mamacita at a dance and it was love at first sight for them, too. But they didn't believe in it and agreed to part ways. Two weeks later, my dad showed up and proposed. So I'm right on time."

"Did she accept?"

"No, but she didn't say no, either. She made him work for it. He had to woo her."

"For how long?"

"A few weeks. But since you haven't said no, I'd be happy to put in the time if that's what it takes. I guess proposing behind a van in the middle of the day with my whole family milling around isn't very romantic. I can do better, I can—"

"Be quiet." She slid her arms around his neck. "Be quiet and kiss me."

He did. He most certainly did. In under three seconds she was plastered against him, her hands in his hair, her body aching for more.

"Hey, guys, I was sent to see if that hat on the roof is—whoa!"

Monty ended the kiss, but slowly. He loosened his hold but didn't let go as he locked his gaze with hers. "It's a signal, Rio. I'm trying to get Zinnia to marry me."

"If I may make a suggestion, you should climb into the van. You might have more success."

"Thanks for the tip, little brother. Is Tex with you?"

"No, he's busy passing out brownies. We all decided brownies are perfectly appropriate for breakfast. But they're going fast. Want me to save you some?"

"I still have the ones Tex gave me."

"Zinnia? Want me to set some aside?"

She smiled up at Monty. "No thanks, Rio. I have all I want right here."

"Then I'll be off. Try the van. The back seat folds down. It's—"

"See you later, little brother."

"Yeah, okay. Bye."

Monty tucked her in close again. "What you just said to Rio sounds like I might be getting somewhere. A wooing campaign is still on the table, though. If you—"

"Sounds like a waste of time to me."

"It does?"

"You have a second bedroom, right?"

"Yes, ma'am."

"When I was there for the shoeing, I noticed a couple of extra stalls in the barn."

He tightened his grip. "Is that a yes?"

She gazed up at him, drinking in the love shining in his blue eyes. "It's a hell yes."

He let out a breath. "Thank God. I love you. I love you so much I can't see straight."

"I love you so much I'm throwing out all my rules and going with what my heart tells me."

"And what is your heart saying, pretty lady?"

"That you're a safe bet for me and Tex."

"I am." His gaze was steady. "I gots you."

She smiled. "I gots you, too, Montgomery Bridger."

Snuggling close, she abandoned herself to a kiss that promised a long life filled with joy, love and brownies.

Epilogue

Monty stood in front of a full-length mirror adjusting his string tie. Darn things never did lay right. Next to him, his mini-me tried to adjust his, not easy when he gripped a ring box that he refused to let go of even for a second.

Kneeling down, Monty gave him a hand. Tex's outfit was the same as his — white shirt, embroidered vest, black jeans and boots. Finding adult and kid-sized matching vests had been impossible on short notice. Then Auntie Carmen had offered to make them.

His brothers, who were engaged in a raucous card game behind them, had a similar look. But their vests were a collection of styles and colors — whatever they'd had in their closet. It worked because the bridesmaids and maid of honor had done the same, choosing their favorite summer dresses for the occasion.

"Mommy says you 'dopted me."

"That's right, sport." He undid Tex's string tie and started over. "It's official. You're my son."

"And you're my daddy?"

His throat tightened. "Sure am." The responsibility he'd feared was now a treasured privilege.

"Daddy Mister Monty."

He chuckled. "That's quite a mouthful."

"I don't gots it in my *mouth*."

"I mean it's kinda long."

"I know. Can I just say Daddy?"

"You can." Much more of this and he was liable to start bawling. "Okay, your string tie is looking good. See what you think." Taking him by the shoulders, he turned him toward the mirror.

"Yep. That works. Thanks, Daddy."

He gulped. Such simple words. Packed a punch. He cleared his throat. "You're welcome, son."

Tex popped open the ring box. "Still there."

"So they are." Zinnia had convinced him that an engagement ring was silly when she wouldn't be able to wear it much considering her job. Neither of them would wear their wedding bands during work hours, either.

But he loved what they represented. A Celtic knot etched into the gold surface was identical to the one her parents had chosen for their wedding bands. The symbol of everlasting love gave Zinnia a way to honor their memory and make them a part of the ceremony.

On the inside of each ring was a message special only to him and Zinnia — *I gots you.* He couldn't wait for the moment Tex would hand over that box.

As if in response to his wishes, Pastor Ed rapped on the door. "It's time, gentlemen."

His brothers gathered up the cards and came over to give him and Tex big hugs.

Monty put his hand on Tex's shoulder. "Time to get married, sport."

Tex glanced up, eyes sparkling. "I know."

Leaving the room, they followed Ed, who'd been pastor for as long as Monty could remember, into the crowded chapel. Cole wrapped up the prelude music he'd been providing with his fiddle and Mila joined him to sing Taylor Swift's *Love Story.*

He'd always admired his sister's voice and never more than now. He gazed at the folks—friends, clients, his mom, grandma and aunties—jammed into the pews decorated with multicolored bouquets of zinnias.

They smiled at him, but Tex got most of their adoring attention. He stood ramrod straight, clearly trying to look taller. The Bridger men lined up next to Tex, going in birth order.

This was happening. He was marrying Zinnia today. The rush of happiness made him want to pump his fist in the air and shout for joy.

Instead he focused on his mom. She'd supported his decision from the get-go, and now the unconditional love shining in her eyes put a lump in his throat. His dad was gone, but he had his mom, who was there for him, for all of them.

When Cole and Mila ended the song and launched into Martina McBride's *I Love You*, Monty faced the back of the chapel, his heart rate picking up.

Greta came dancing down the aisle, followed by Claudie, Tracy, Jordan and Mari, each performing whatever steps they'd chosen, each flashing him a grin as they sashayed over to the far side of the altar. By the time they finished up, he was laughing.

Then the tune switched again, to Blake Shelton and Gwen Stefani's *Nobody But You,* and he sucked in a breath. This was it.

Zinnia appeared.

His heart thundered so loud he could barely hear the music or notice that Graham was escorting her. She hadn't let him see the dress, hadn't given him any hints except that she thought he'd like it.

Understatement of the century.

White and filmy, it flowed around her like... like moonlight. He felt cool grass under his bare feet, caught the scent of pine and wild rose. He was marrying the woman walking toward him. He was marrying this goddess of the night.

"Daddy." Tex pulled on his sleeve. "You gots to go over there. Mommy's waiting."

He blinked. Sure enough, the song continued as Zinnia stood smiling at him. Graham had stepped back.

He quickly moved into position. "Sorry," he murmured. "I was... blown away"

"Just what I was going for. Let's do this."

Which they did. Evidently he responded as he was supposed to. Right on cue, Tex produced the rings.

The sight of those gold bands acted like a cool breeze over his fevered brain, leaving him calm and extremely focused. His gaze locked with hers as he slipped the ring on her finger. "I love you, Zinnia. I will always love you."

The glow in her eyes intensified. "I know." She slid the ring on his finger without fumbling, her breathing steady. "I will always love you, Montgomery."

"They gots the rings. Are they married yet?"

Pastor Ed leaned down. "Almost, Tex. I just have to say the magic words."

"Please and thank you?"

He chuckled. "The other magic words." He straightened and smiled. "By the power vested in me, I now pronounce Zinnia and Monty married. Blessing on you and your new family. You may kiss."

Clapping and cheering, the guests rose to their feet as Monty took Zinnia by the shoulders and gave her a slow, deliberate kiss.

Next to him, Tex jumped up and down chanting *ohboyohboyohboy.*

Monty couldn't have said it better. When at last he let go, Zinnia's eyes were sparkling.

Her lips moved in a silent *No fair.*

He lowered his voice. "Catch you later." Tex would be with Mari and Graham tonight.

But in this moment, he needed to give that little cowpoke a hug. Hoisting him up, he absorbed the happiness in Tex's big ol' smile. "Guess what, son?"

"You and Mommy are married! *Finally.*"

Made him chuckle considering they'd thrown this wedding together in a couple of weeks. But he agreed with Tex. He'd been chomping at the bit, too.

"It's not only about your mommy and me, though. Our marriage turns the three of us into a family."

"I know. Now I gots a Mommy *and* a Daddy."

"And we've got you." Zinnia wrapped her arms around them, closing the circle. "Perfect."

"Yep." Tex nodded. "Perfect." Then he paused to study them. "But I gots to have a baby sister."

Monty choked on a laugh. He and Zin had been busy and there was a good chance she was already pregnant. Did the kid have a sixth sense?

He held Zinnia's gaze. "Think that could be arranged?"

"I do." Her eyes glowed with the joy of a shared secret.

"Then let's see what the future brings." For the first time in his life, he couldn't wait to find out.

New York Times bestselling author Vicki Lewis Thompson's love affair with cowboys started with the Lone Ranger, continued through Maverick, and took a turn south of the border with Zorro. She views cowboys as the Western version of knights in shining armor, rugged men who value honor, honesty and hard work. Fortunately for her, she lives in the Arizona desert, where broad-shouldered, lean-hipped cowboys abound. Blessed with such an abundance of inspiration, she only hopes that she can do them justice.

For more information about this prolific author, visit her website and sign up for her newsletter. She loves connecting with readers.

VickiLewisThompson.com

www.ingramcontent.com/pod-product-compliance
Lightning Source LLC
Chambersburg PA
CBHW032002050726
47590CB00006B/2020

* 9 7 8 1 6 3 8 0 3 8 6 5 8 *